Mighty Mighty MONSTERS

# THE WOLF BOY'S WISH

STONE ARCH BOOKS
a capstone imprint

Mighty Mighty Monsters are published by
Stone Arch Books, A Capstone Imprint, 1710 Roe
Crest Drive, North Mankato, Minnesota 56003
www.capstonepub.com



Library of Congress Cataloging-in-Publication
Data
O'Reilly, Sean, 1974-
The wolfboy's wish / by Sean O'Reilly ;
illustrated by Arcana Studio.
p. cm. -- (Mighty Mighty Monsters)
Summary: When he discovers a magic lamp with
a wish-granting genie inside, Talbot the werewolf
sees a chance to get out of summer school and
his homework assignment.
ISBN-13: 978-1-4342-3219-9 (library binding)
ISBN-10: 1-4342-3219-0 (library binding)
ISBN-13: 978-1-4342-4613-4 (paperback)
1. Graphic novels. [1. Graphic novels. 2.
Monsters--Fiction. 3. Werewolves--Fiction. 4.
Homework--Fiction. 5. Responsibility--Fiction.]
I. Arcana Studio. II. Title.
PZ7.7.O74Wo 2011
741.5'973--dc22

2011003445

Printed in the United States of America
in North Mankato, Minnesota.
052013
007366R

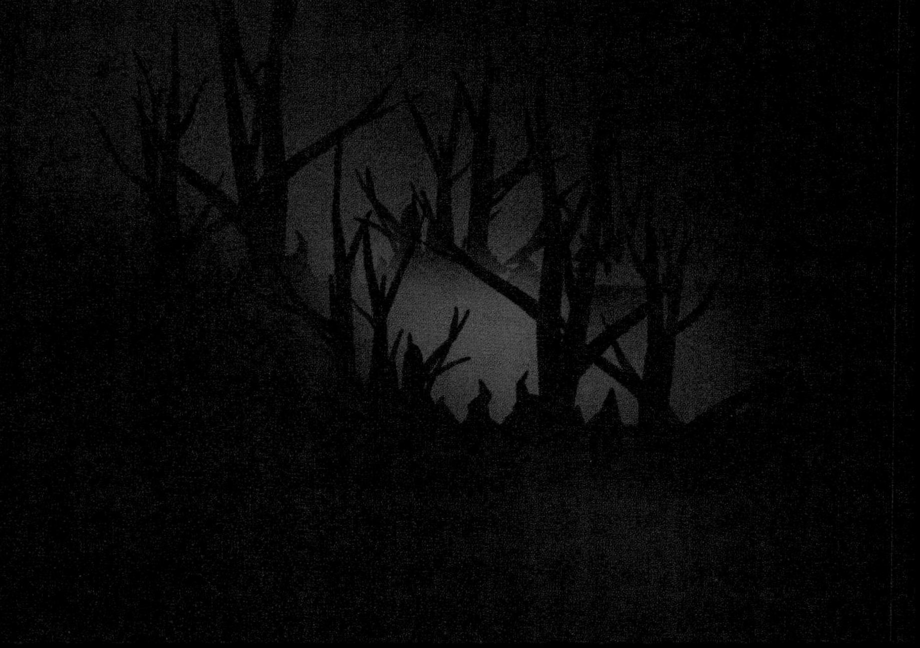

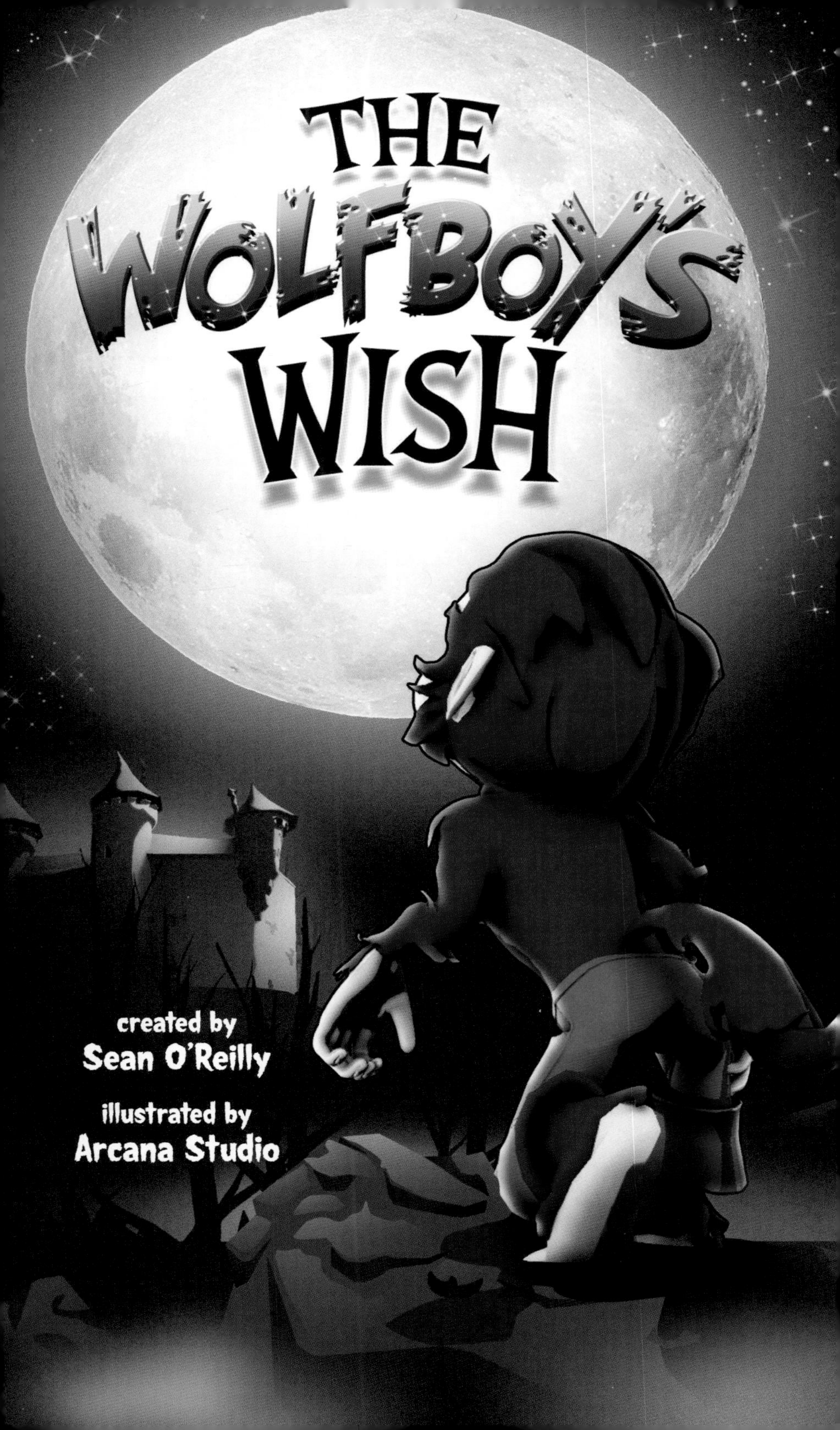
THE
WOLFBOY'S
WISH
created by
Sean O'Reilly
illustrated by
Arcana Studio

In a strange corner of the world known as Transylmania . . .

Legendary monsters were born

WELCOME TO TRANSYLMANIA

But long before their frightful fame, these classic creatures faced fears of their own.

o take on terrifying teachers and homework horrors,
hey formed the most fearsome friendship on Earth . . .

Mighty
Mighty
MONSTERS

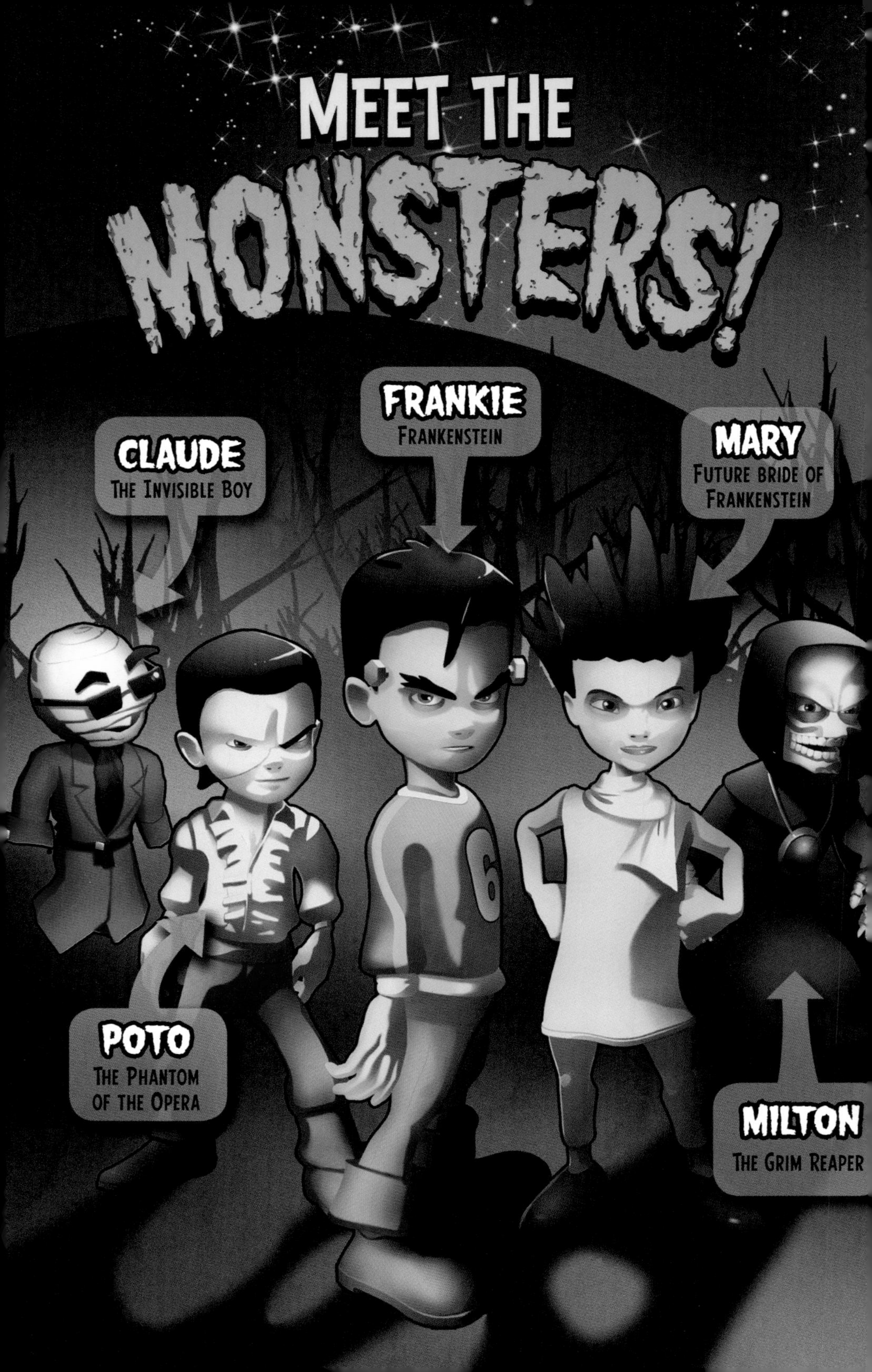
MEET THE
MONSTERS!
FRANKIE
FRANKENSTEIN
CLAUDE
THE INVISIBLE BOY
MARY
FUTURE BRIDE OF FRANKENSTEIN
POTO
THE PHANTOM OF THE OPERA
MILTON
THE GRIM REAPER

KITSUNE
THE FOX GIRL
TALBOT
THE WOLFBOY
IGOR
THE HUNCHBACK
VLAD
DRACULA
WITCHITA
THE WITCH

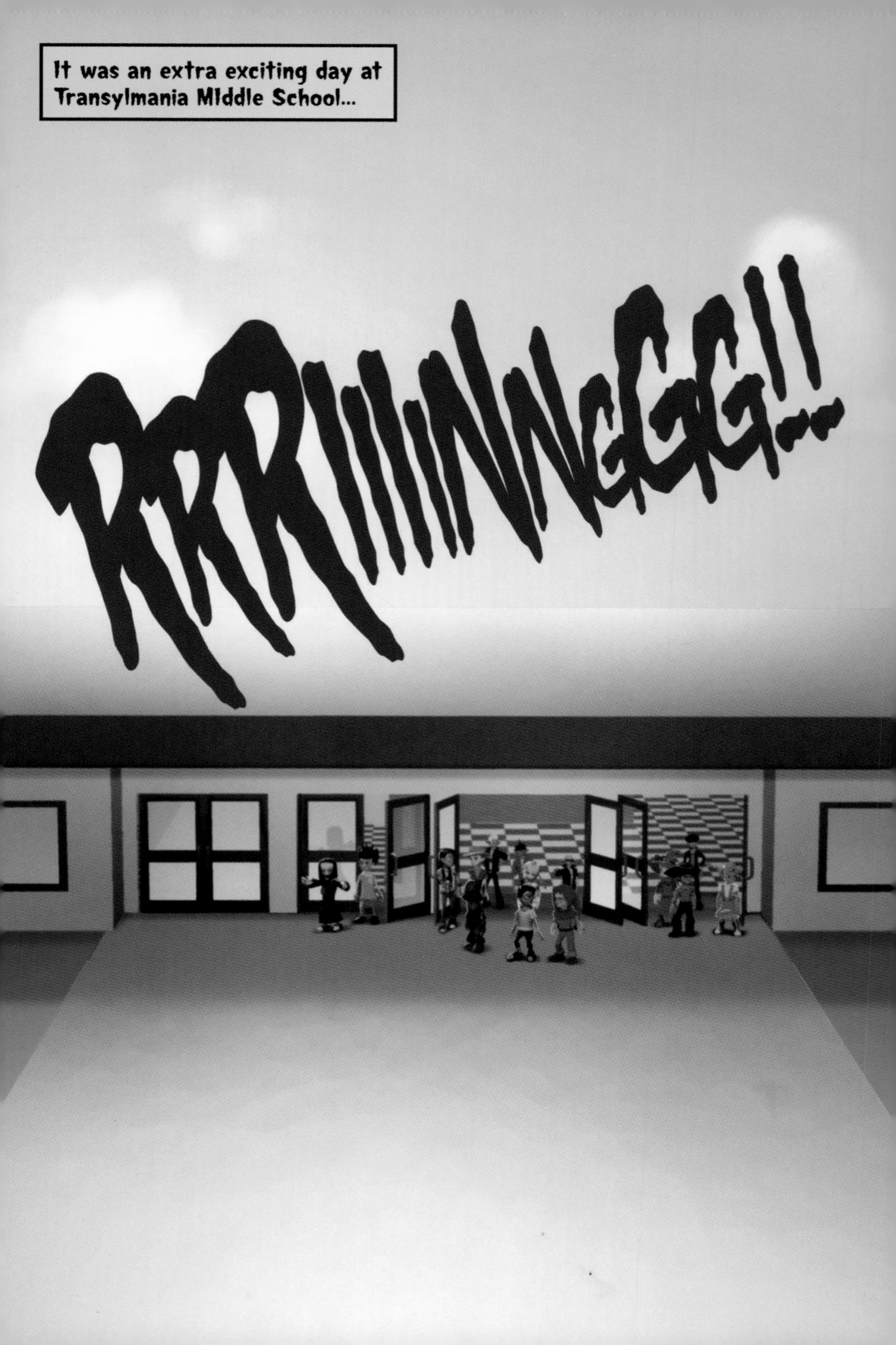
It was an extra exciting day at Transylmania MIddle School...
RRRIIIINNGGG!!...

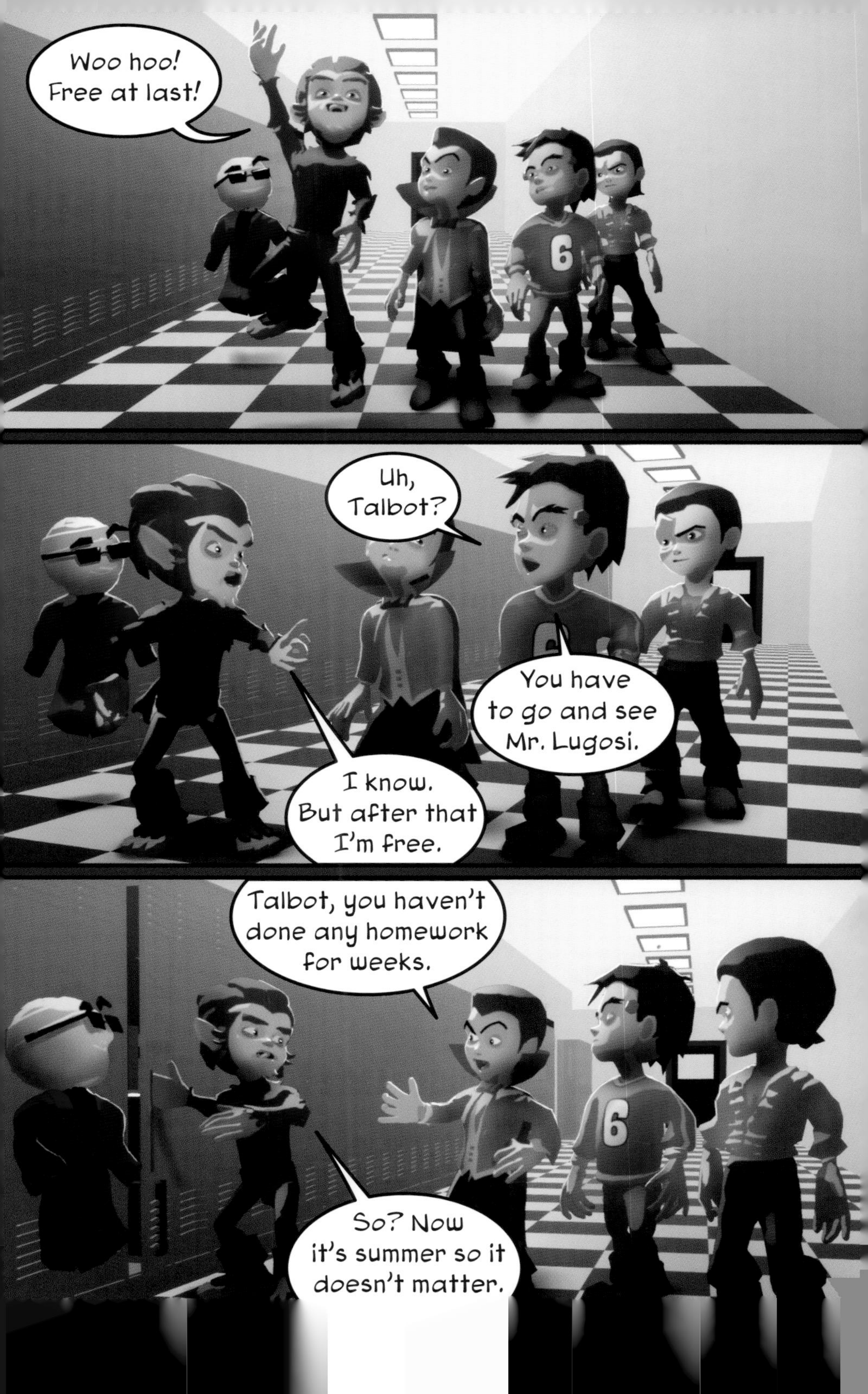
Woo hoo! Free at last!
Uh, Talbot?
You have to go and see Mr. Lugosi.
I know. But after that I'm free.
Talbot, you haven't done any homework for weeks.
So? Now it's summer so it doesn't matter.

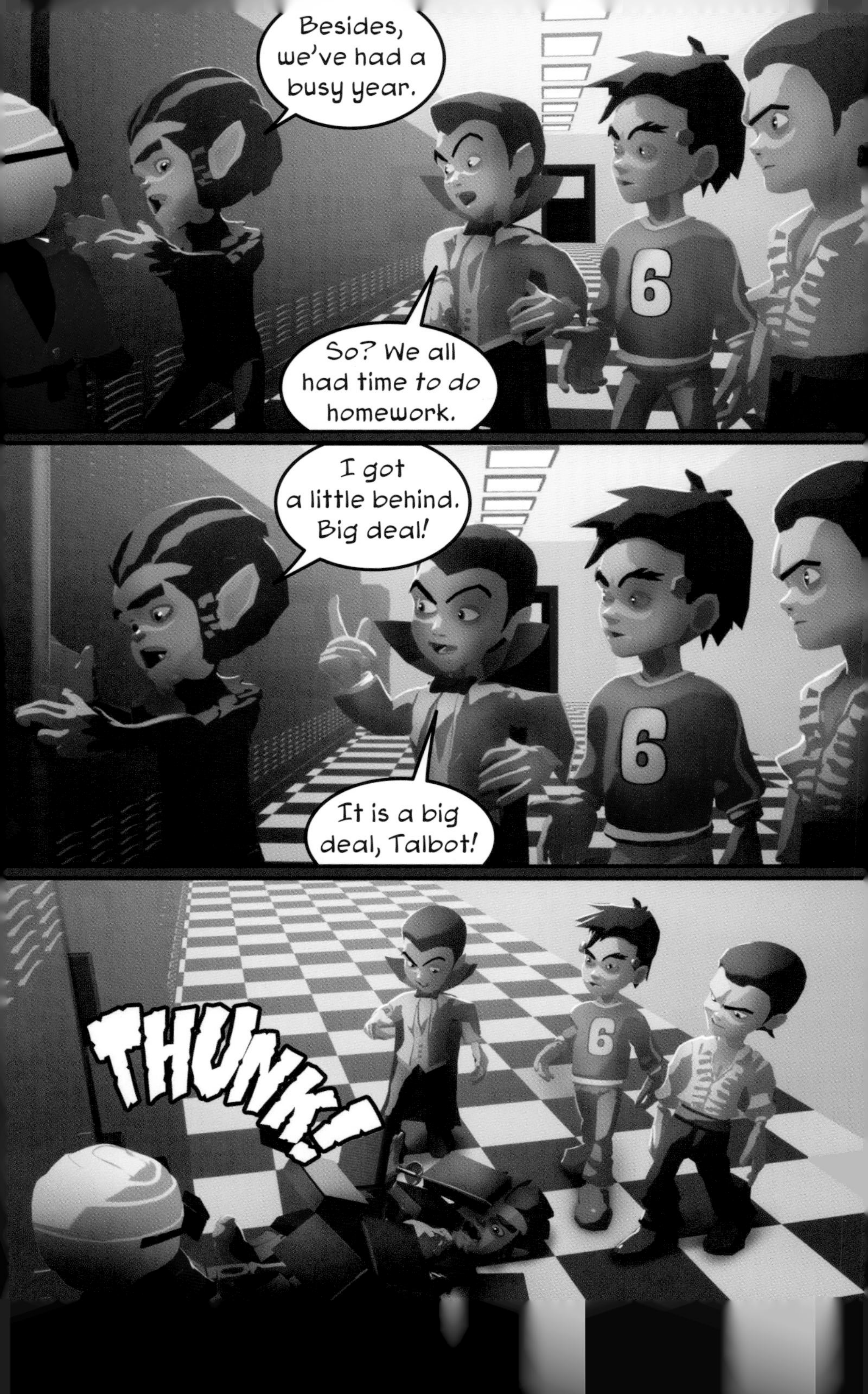
Besides, we've had a busy year.
So? We all had time to do homework.
I got a little behind. Big deal!
It is a big deal, Talbot!
THUNK!

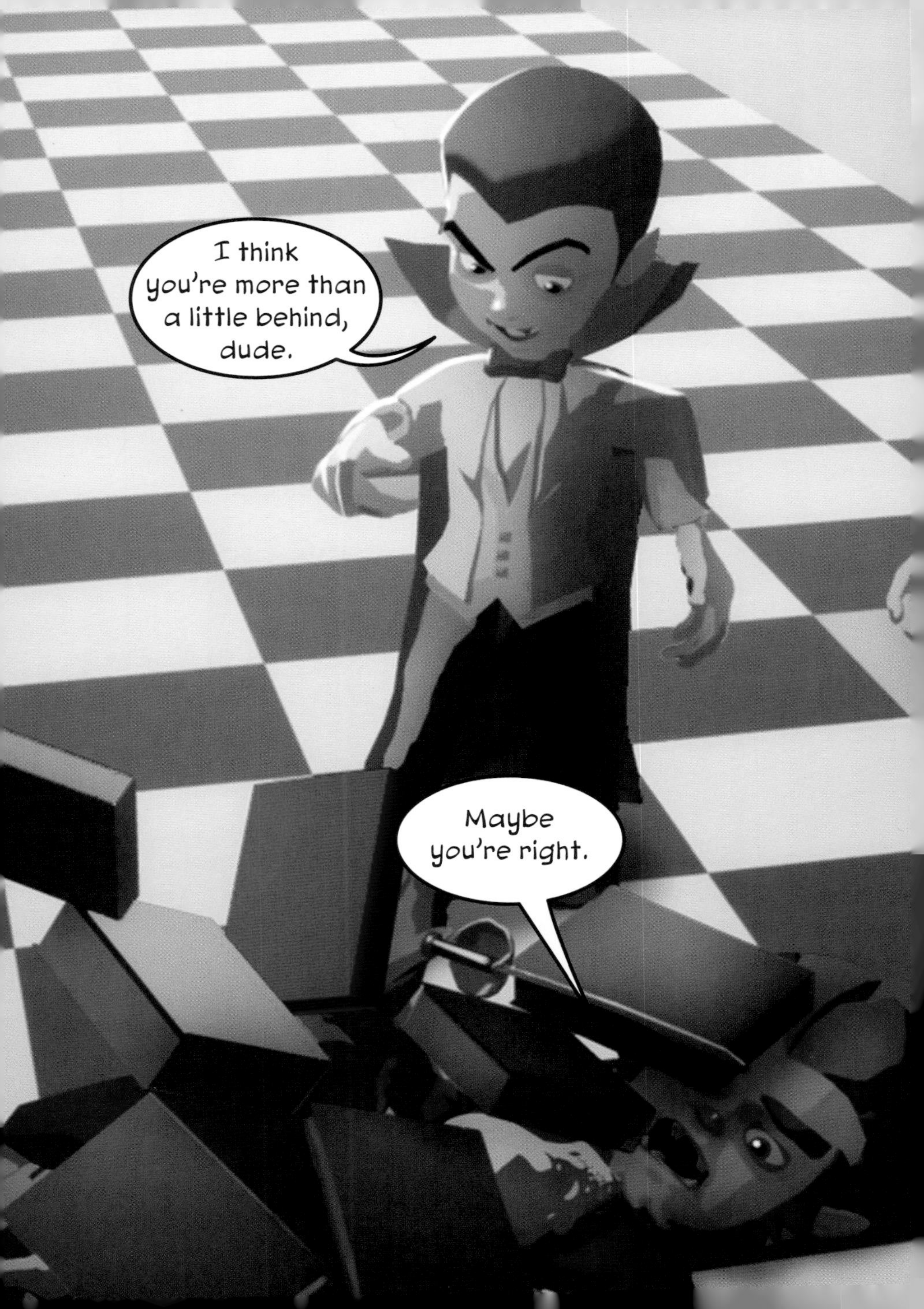
I think you're more than a little behind, dude.
Maybe you're right.

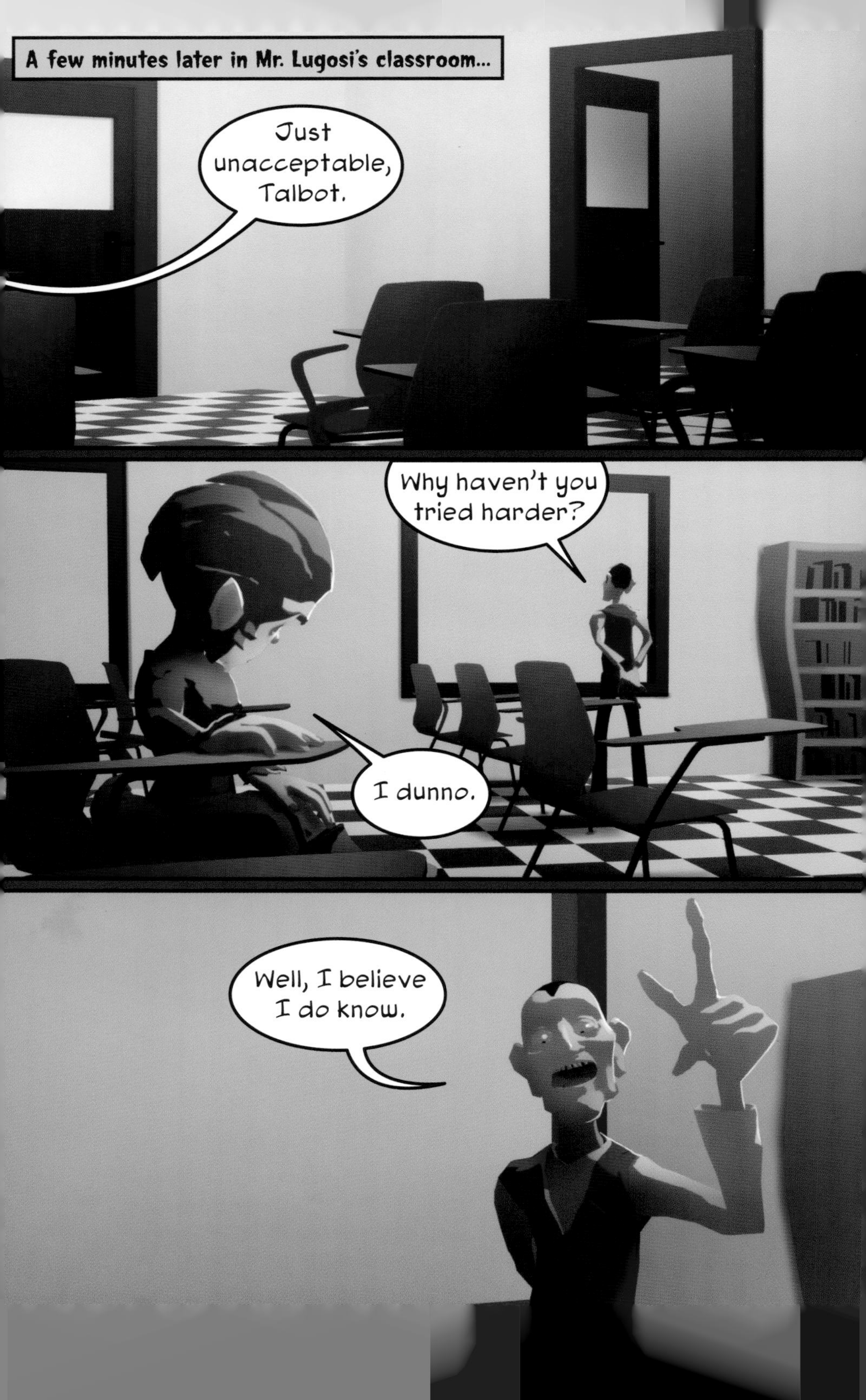
A few minutes later in Mr. Lugosi's classroom...
Just unacceptable, Talbot.
Why haven't you tried harder?
I dunno.
Well, I believe I do know.

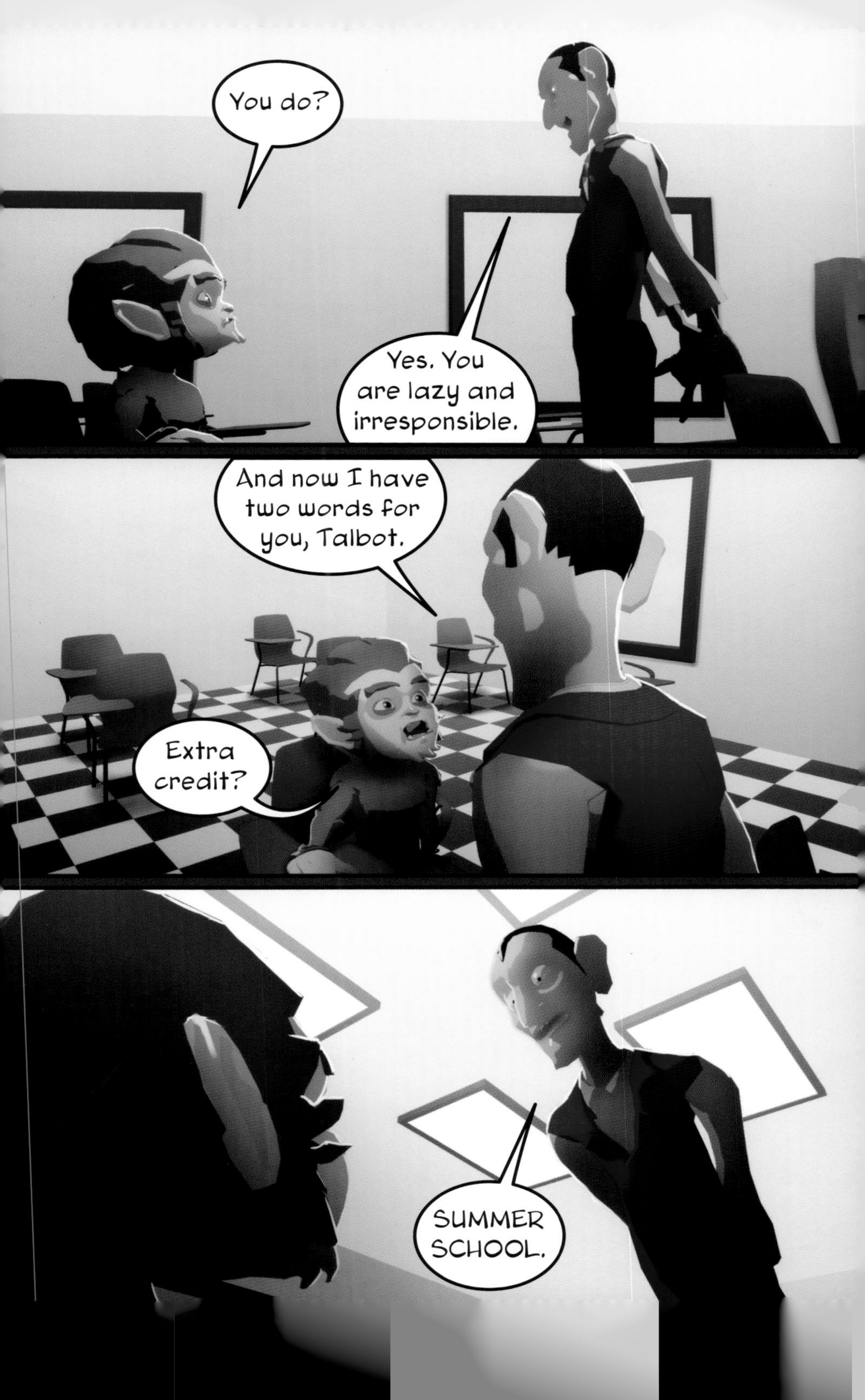
You do?
Yes. You are lazy and irresponsible.
And now I have two words for you, Talbot.
Extra credit?
SUMMER SCHOOL.

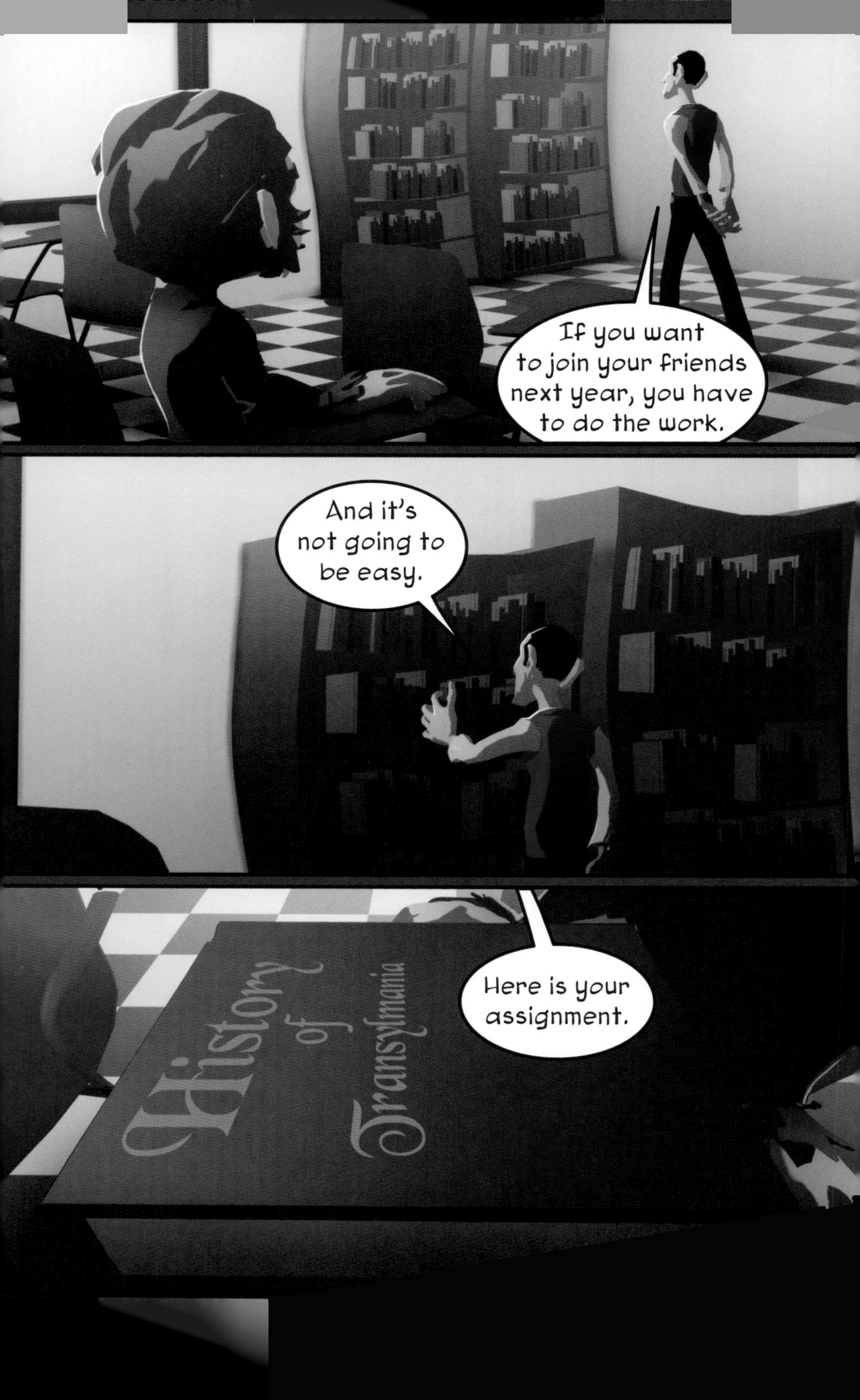
If you want to join your friends next year, you have to do the work.
And it's not going to be easy.
History of Transylmania
Here is your assignment.

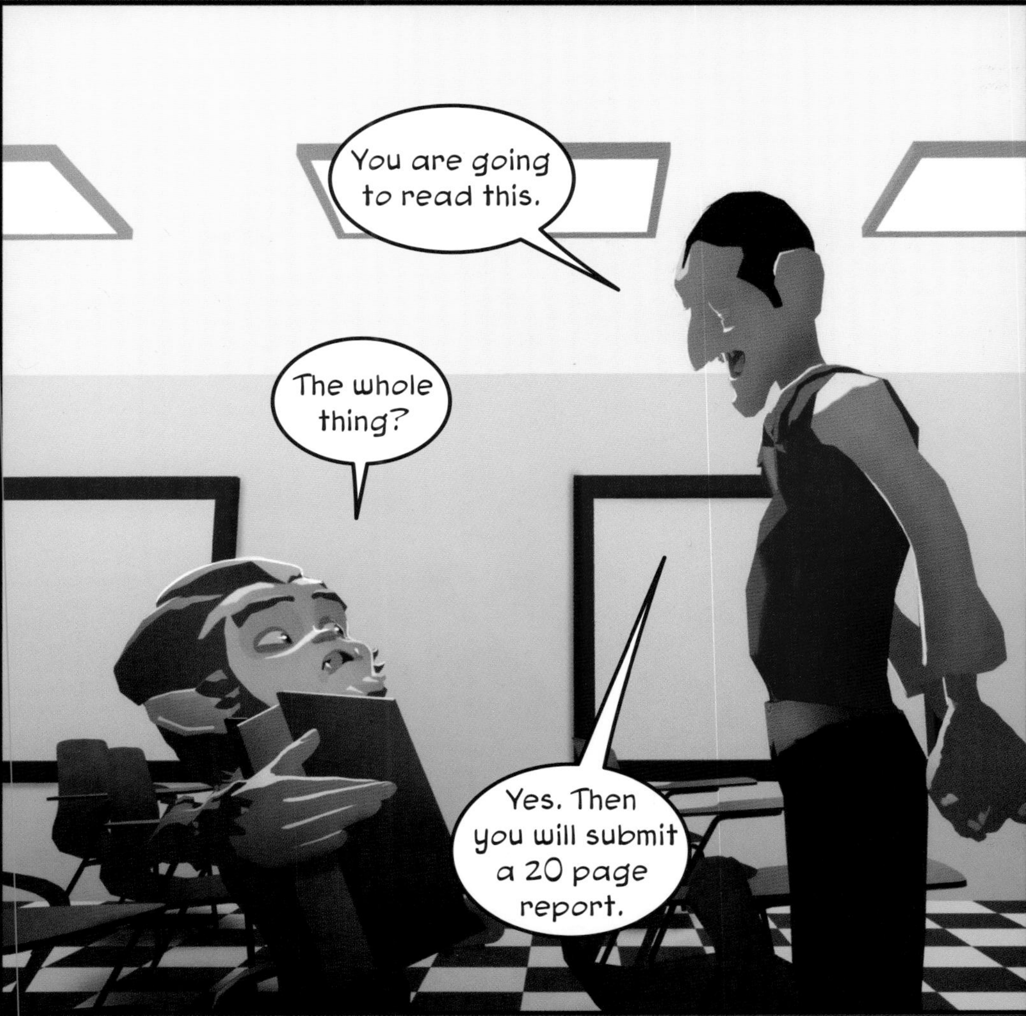
You are going to read this.
The whole thing?
Yes. Then you will submit a 20 page report.

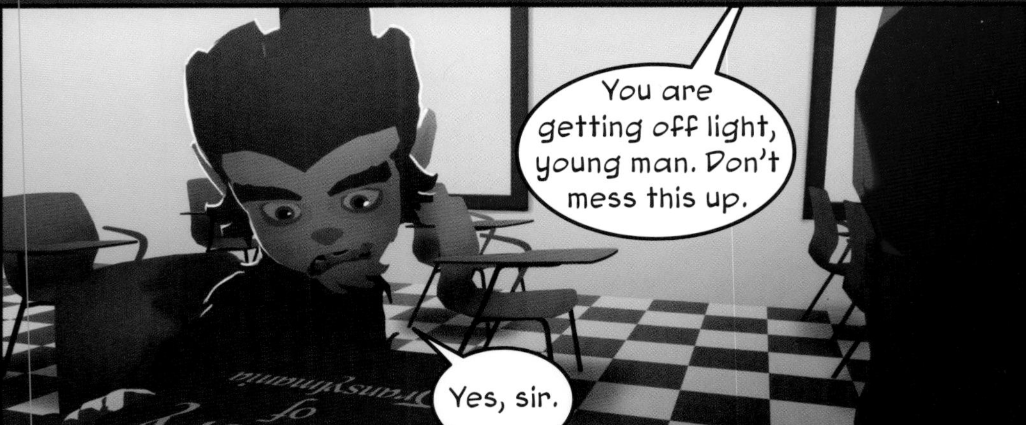
You are getting off light, young man. Don't mess this up.
Yes, sir.

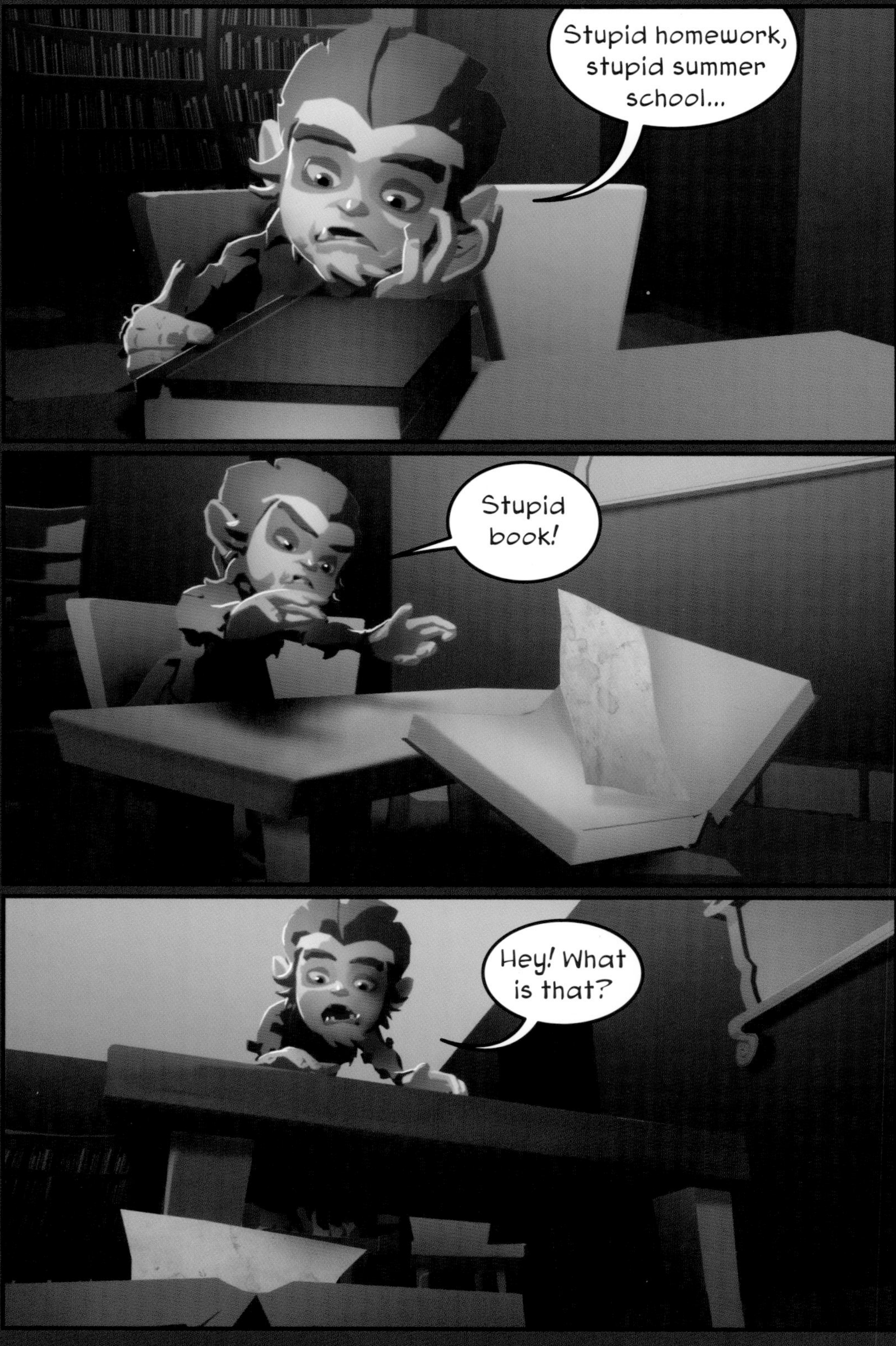
Stupid homework, stupid summer school...
Stupid book!
Hey! What is that?

To whoever finds this map, I say thee welcome to it. Its mysteries are yours to unfold, and the prize within yours to do with as you will. Spend wisely what you find there.

**Know this:** Any attempt you make to reach this treasure, you must make alone. Tempt not others with your quest. Its prize is meant only for you.

Good luck!

Silas V. Suvious

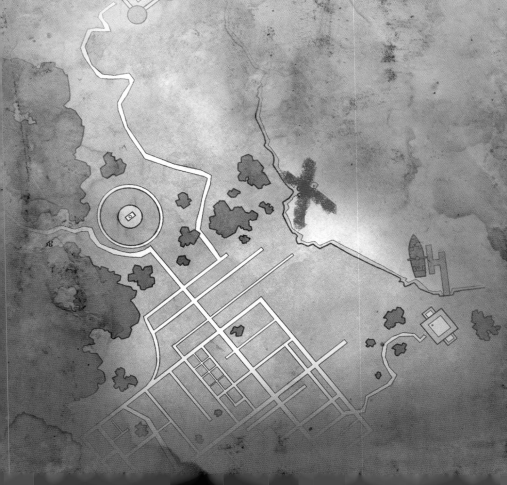

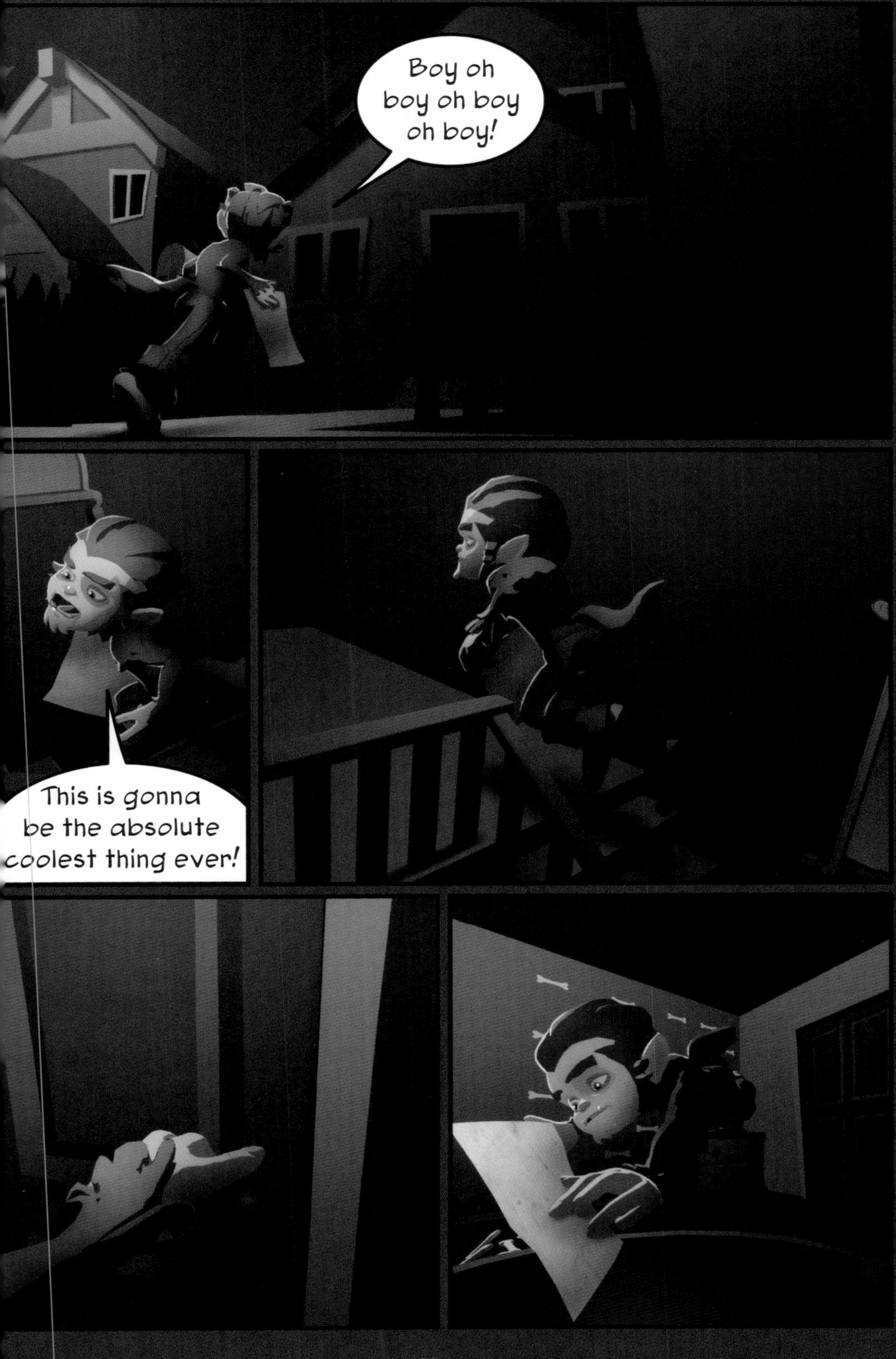
Boy oh boy oh boy oh boy!
This is gonna be the absolute coolest thing ever!

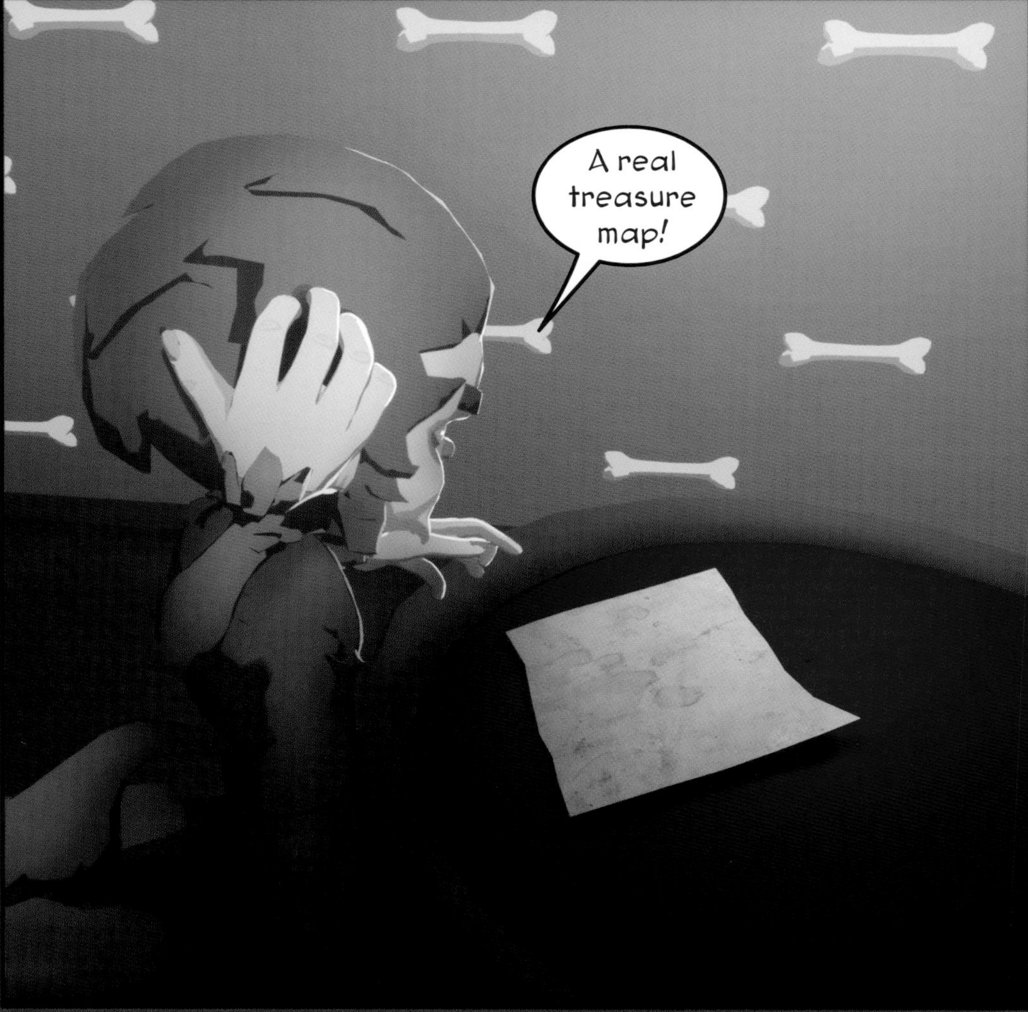
A real treasure map!

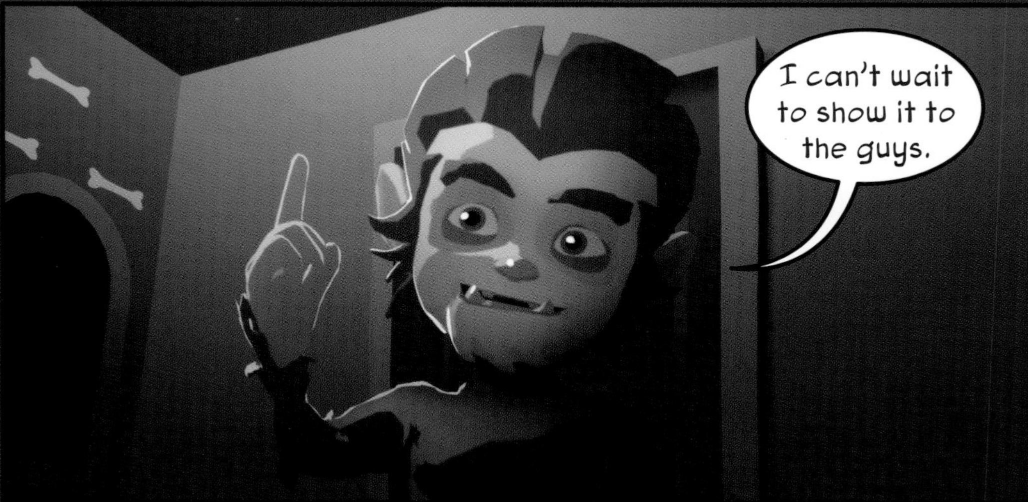
I can't wait to show it to the guys.

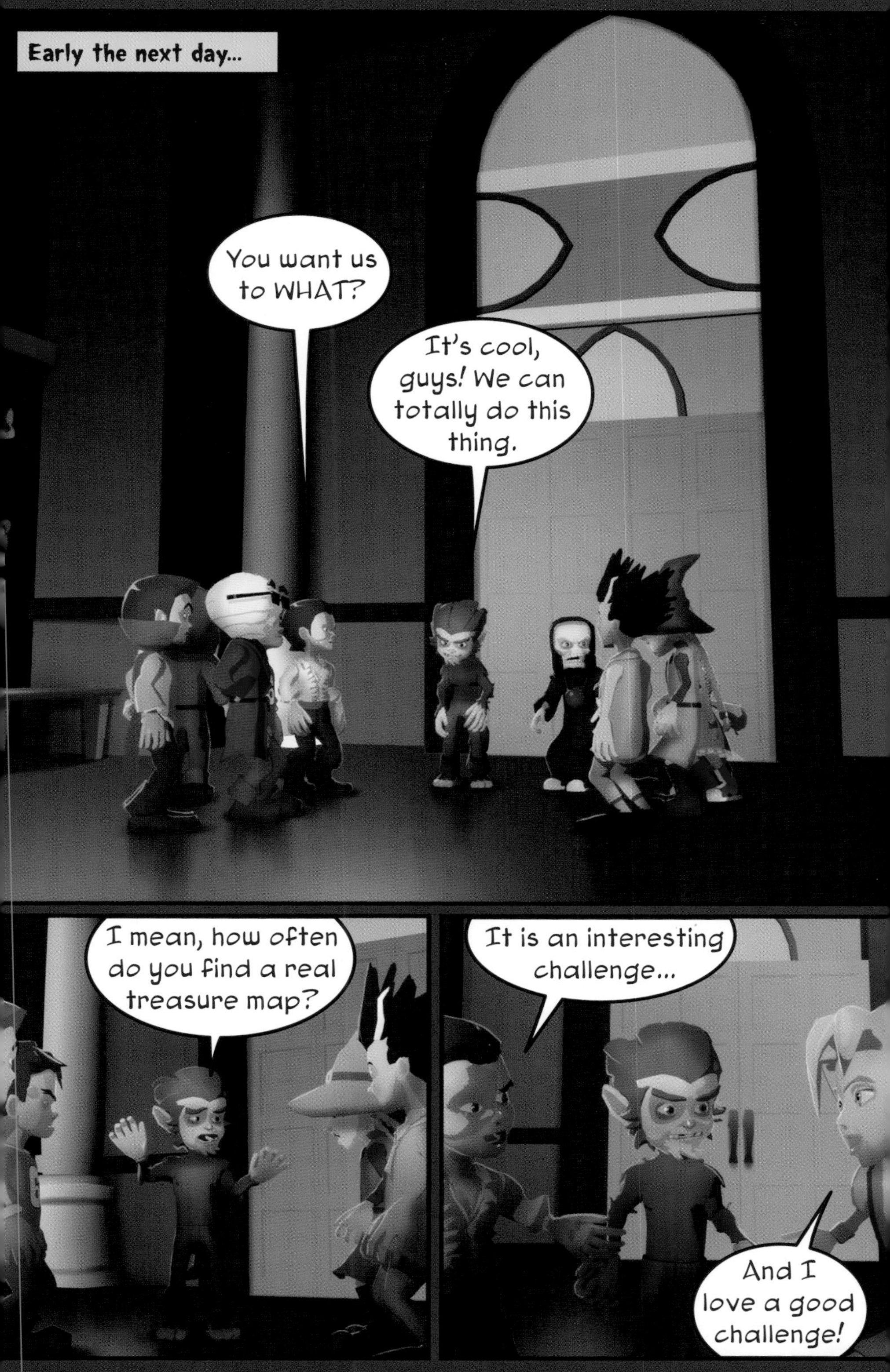
Early the next day...
You want us to WHAT?
It's cool, guys! We can totally do this thing.
I mean, how often do you find a real treasure map?
It is an interesting challenge...
And I love a good challenge!

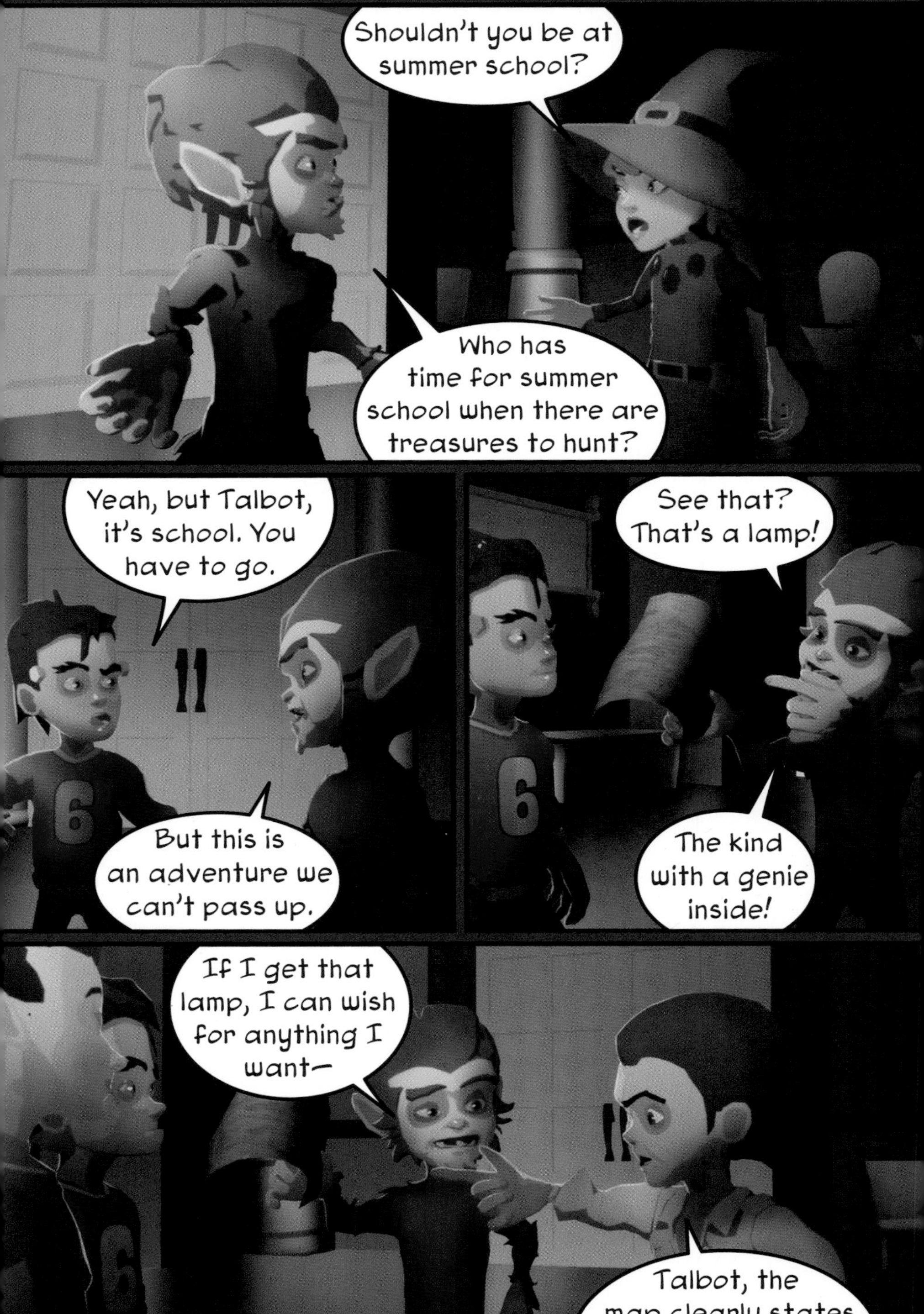
Shouldn't you be at summer school?
Who has time for summer school when there are treasures to hunt?
Yeah, but Talbot, it's school. You have to go.
But this is an adventure we can't pass up.
See that? That's a lamp!
The kind with a genie inside!
If I get that lamp, I can wish for anything I want—
Talbot, the map clearly states you are to pursue this quest by yourself.

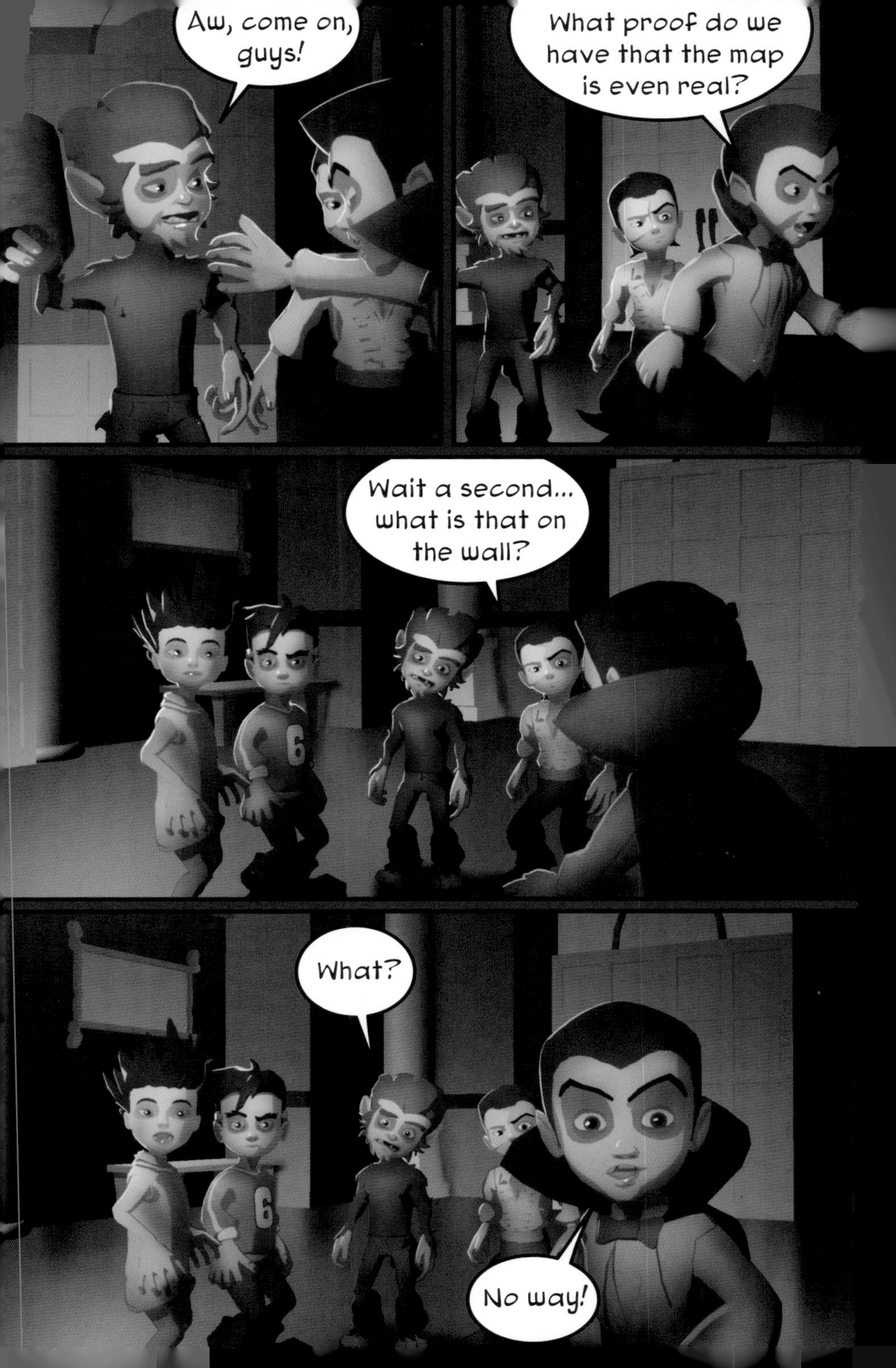
Aw, come on, guys!
What proof do we have that the map is even real?
Wait a second... what is that on the wall?
What?
No way!

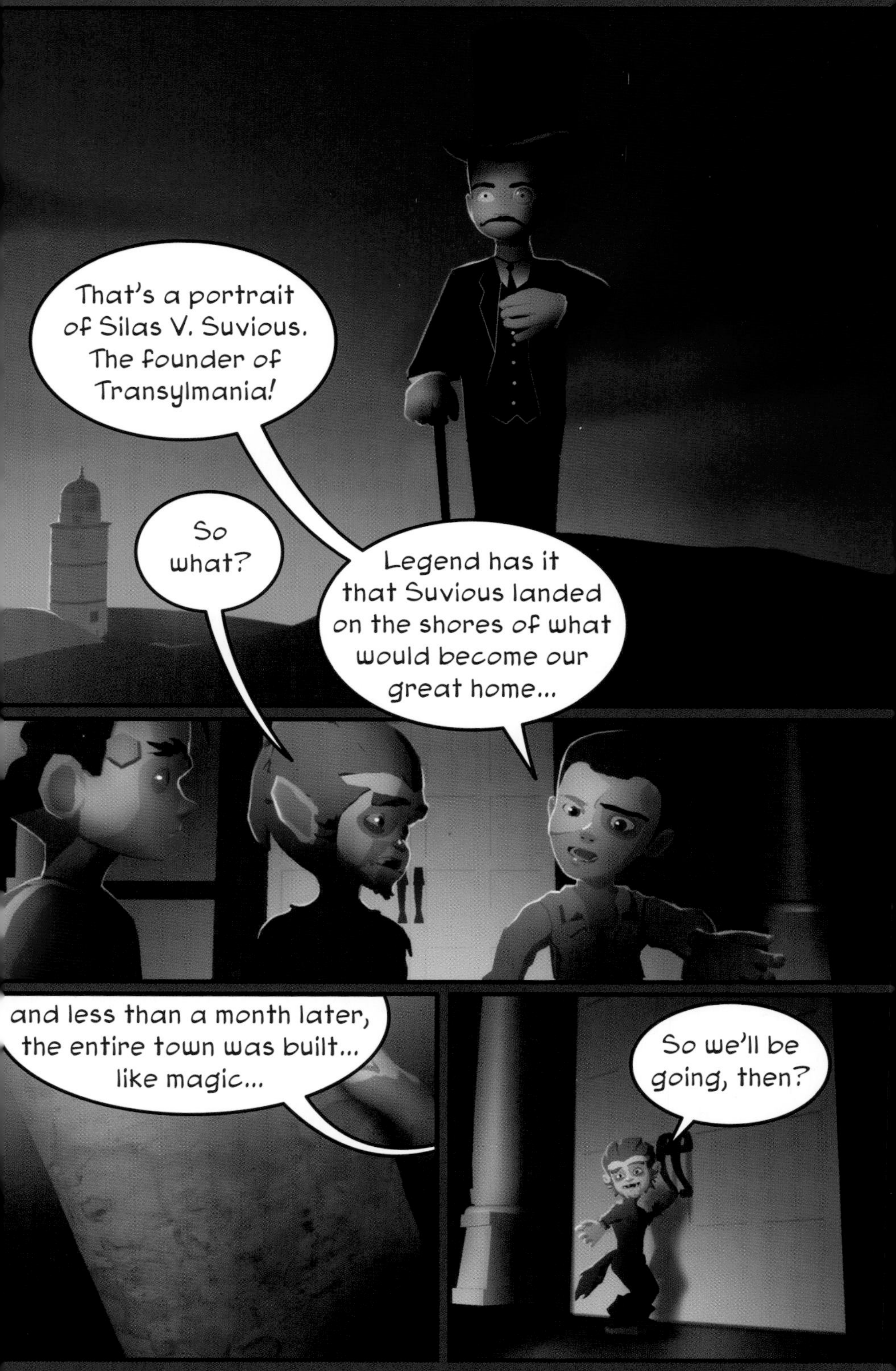
That's a portrait of Silas V. Suvious. The founder of Transylmania!
So what?
Legend has it that Suvious landed on the shores of what would become our great home...
and less than a month later, the entire town was built... like magic...
So we'll be going, then?

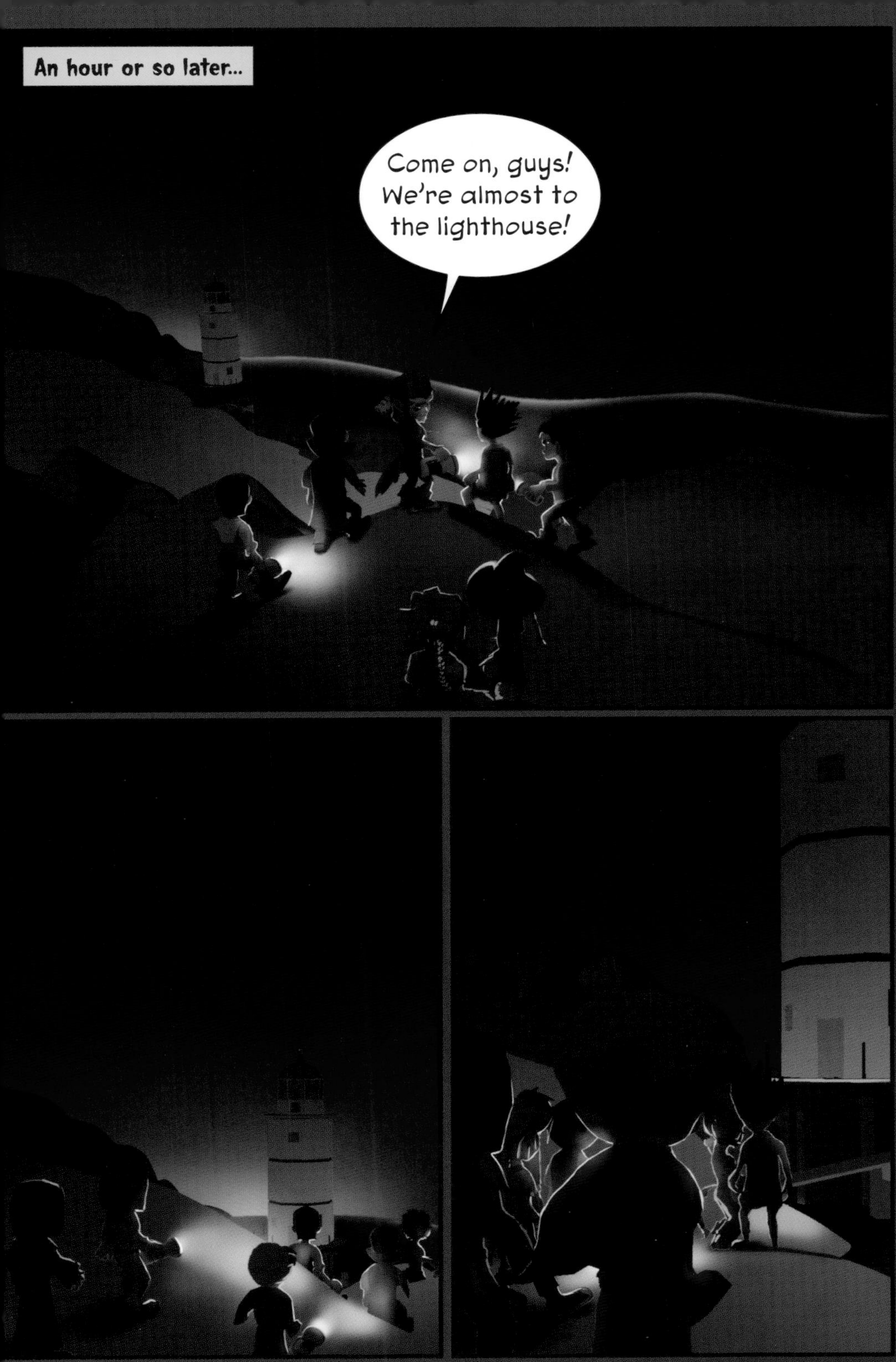
An hour or so later...
Come on, guys! We're almost to the lighthouse!

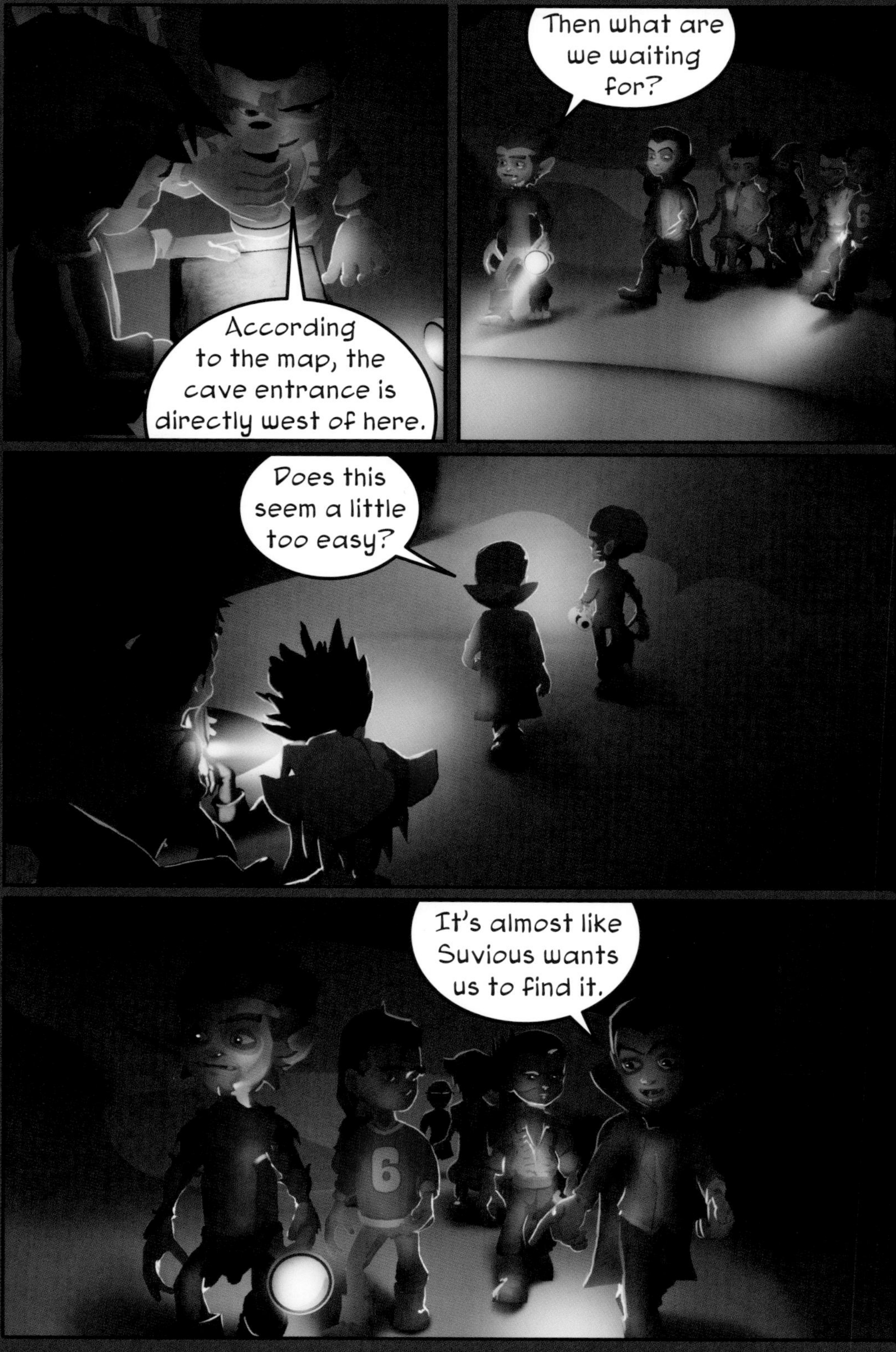
According to the map, the cave entrance is directly west of here.
Then what are we waiting for?
Does this seem a little too easy?
It's almost like Suvious wants us to find it.

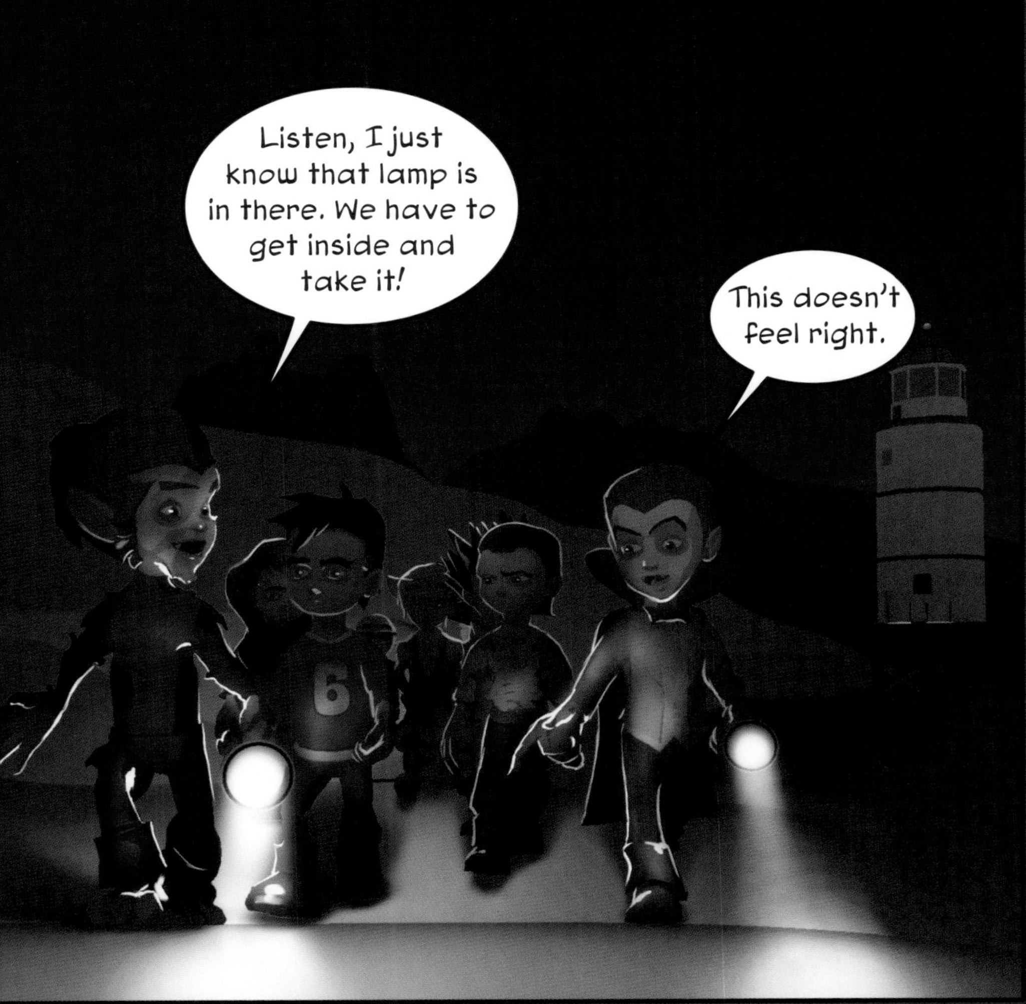
Listen, I just know that lamp is in there. We have to get inside and take it!
This doesn't feel right.

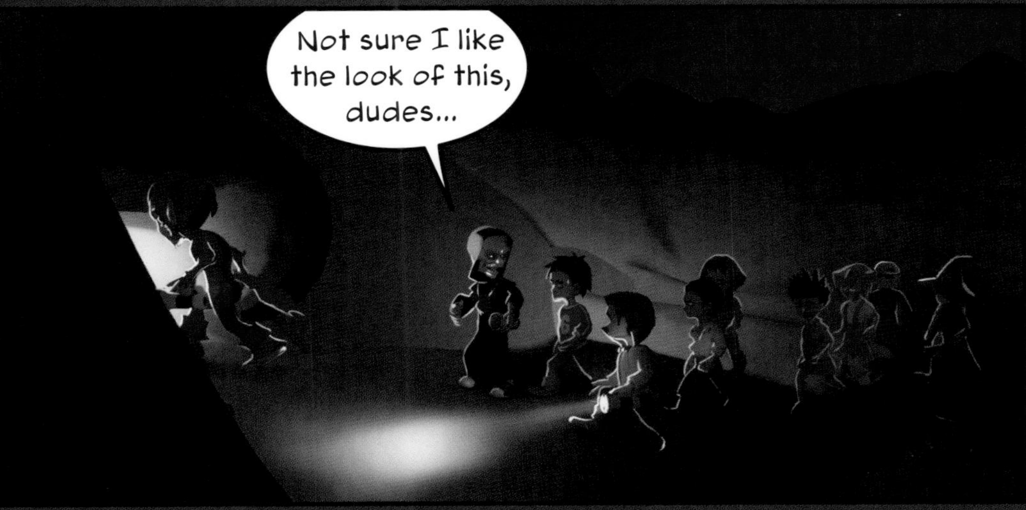
Not sure I like the look of this, dudes...

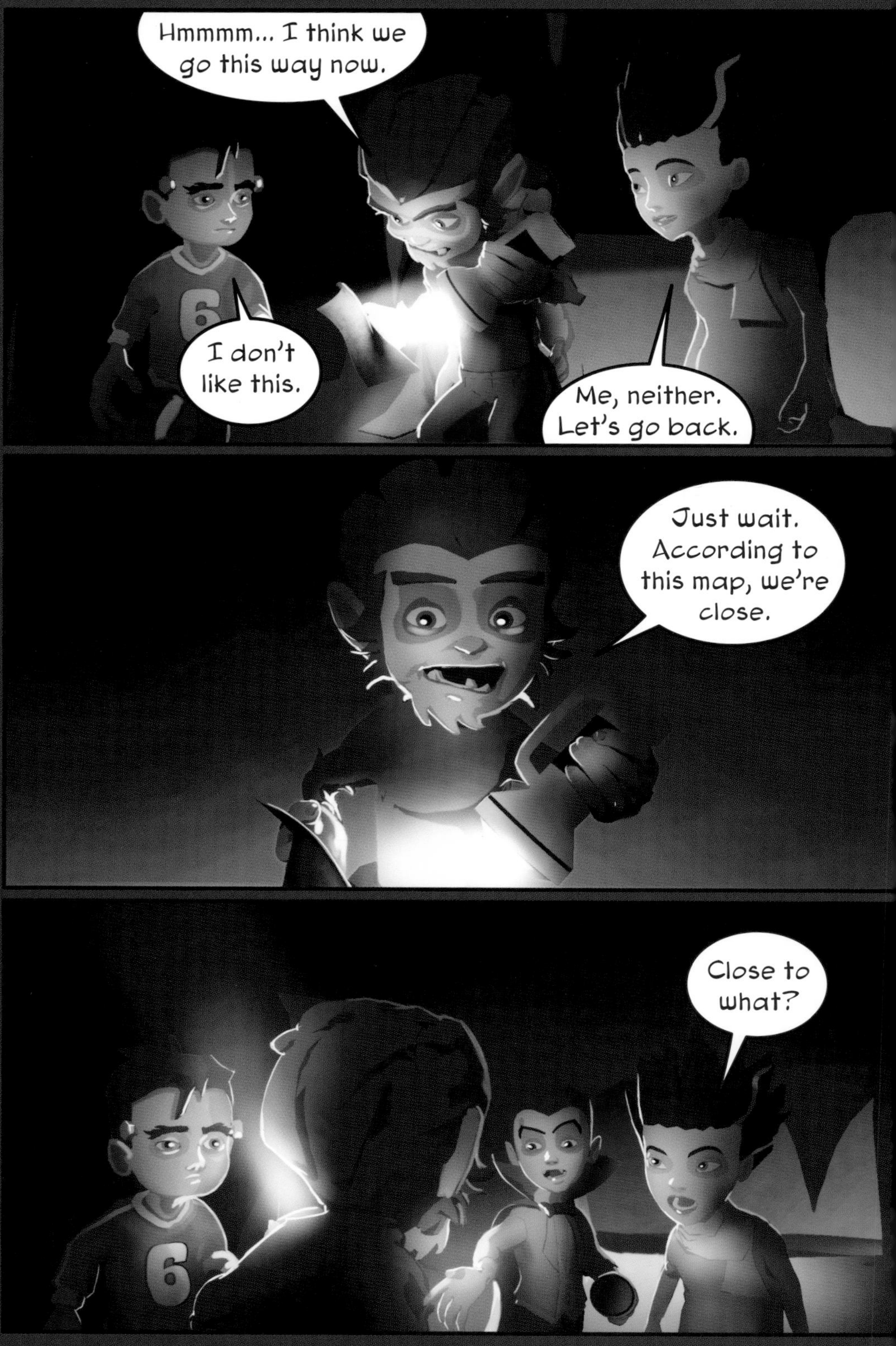
Hmmmm... I think we go this way now.
I don't like this.
Me, neither. Let's go back.
Just wait. According to this map, we're close.
Close to what?

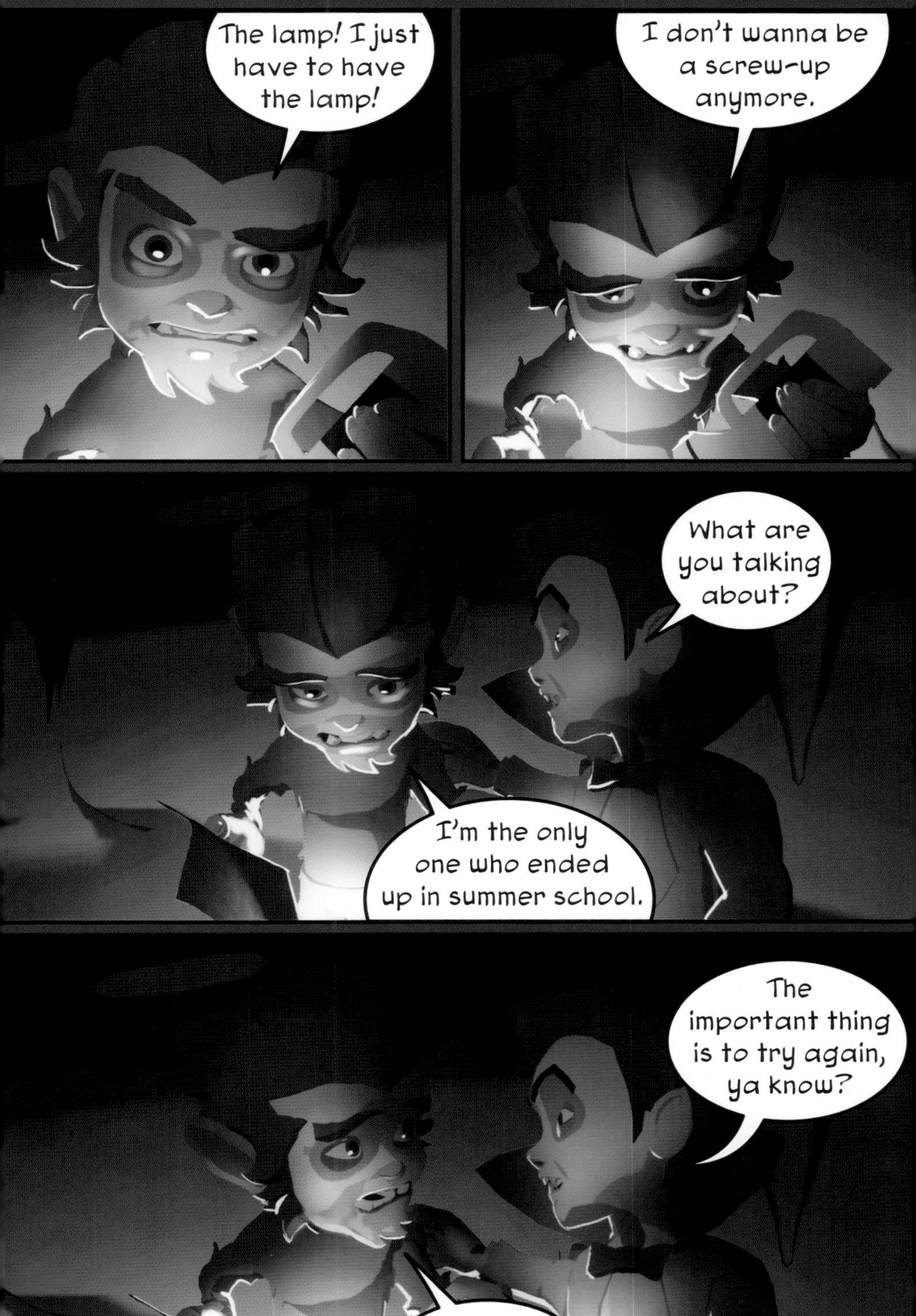
The lamp! I just have to have the lamp!
I don't wanna be a screw-up anymore.
What are you talking about?
I'm the only one who ended up in summer school.
The important thing is to try again, ya know?
I know. But it's hard.

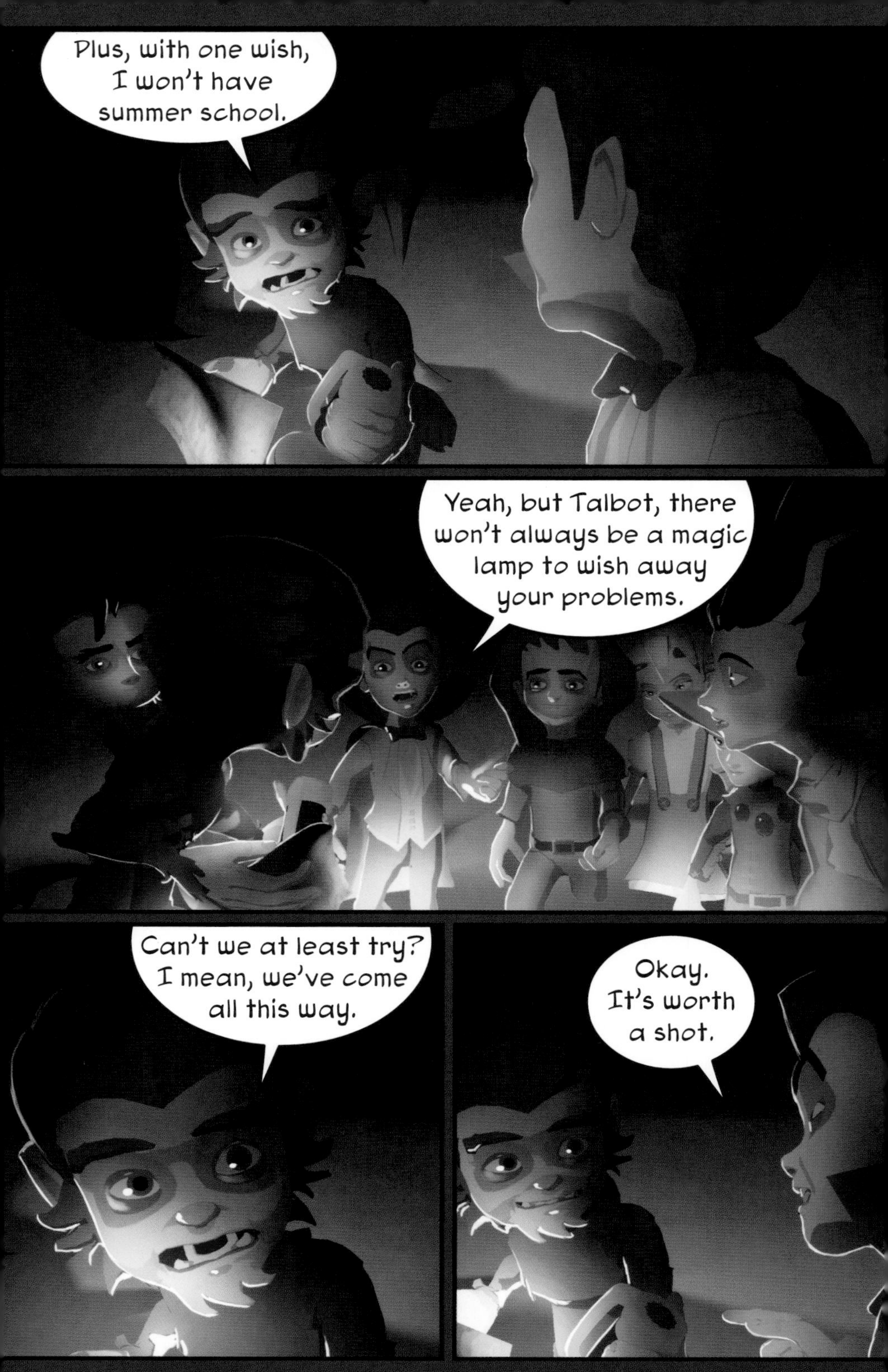
Plus, with one wish, I won't have summer school.
Yeah, but Talbot, there won't always be a magic lamp to wish away your problems.
Can't we at least try? I mean, we've come all this way.
Okay. It's worth a shot.

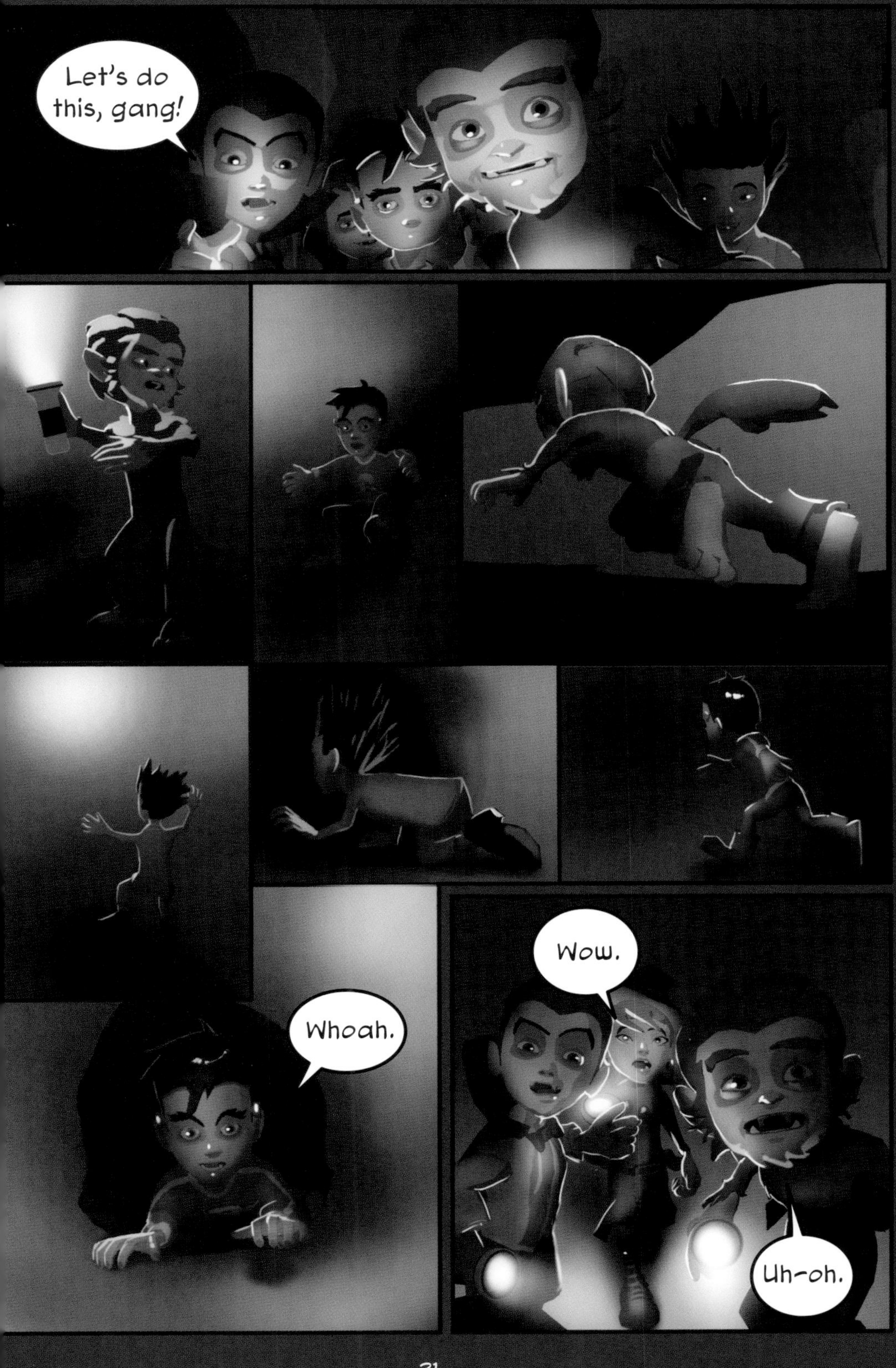

Let's do this, gang!
Whoah.
Wow.
Uh-oh.

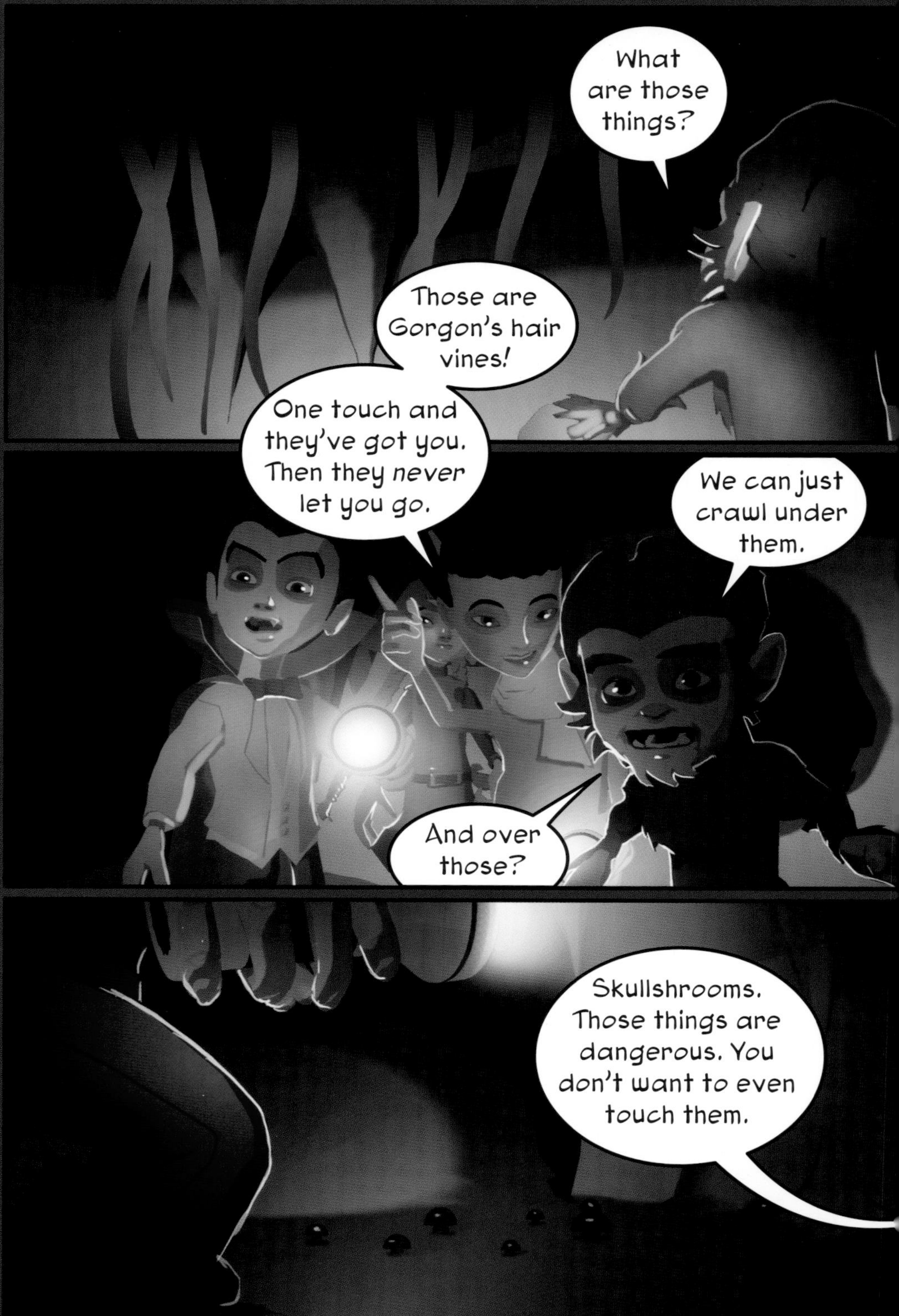
What are those things?
Those are Gorgon's hair vines!
One touch and they've got you. Then they *never* let you go.
We can just crawl under them.
And over those?
Skullshrooms. Those things are dangerous. You don't want to even touch them.

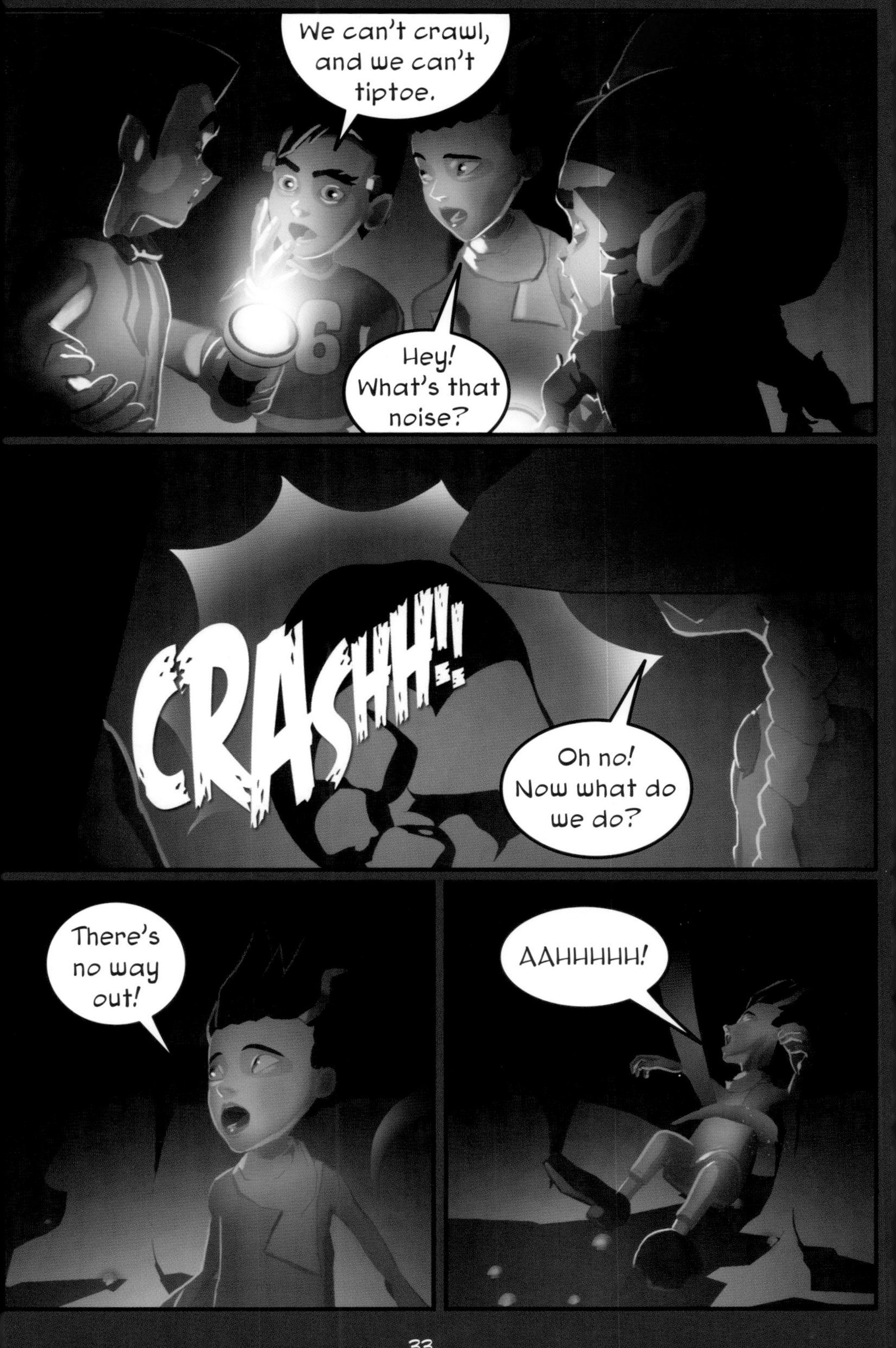
We can't crawl, and we can't tiptoe.
Hey! What's that noise?
CRASHH!!
Oh no! Now what do we do?
There's no way out!
AAHHHHH!

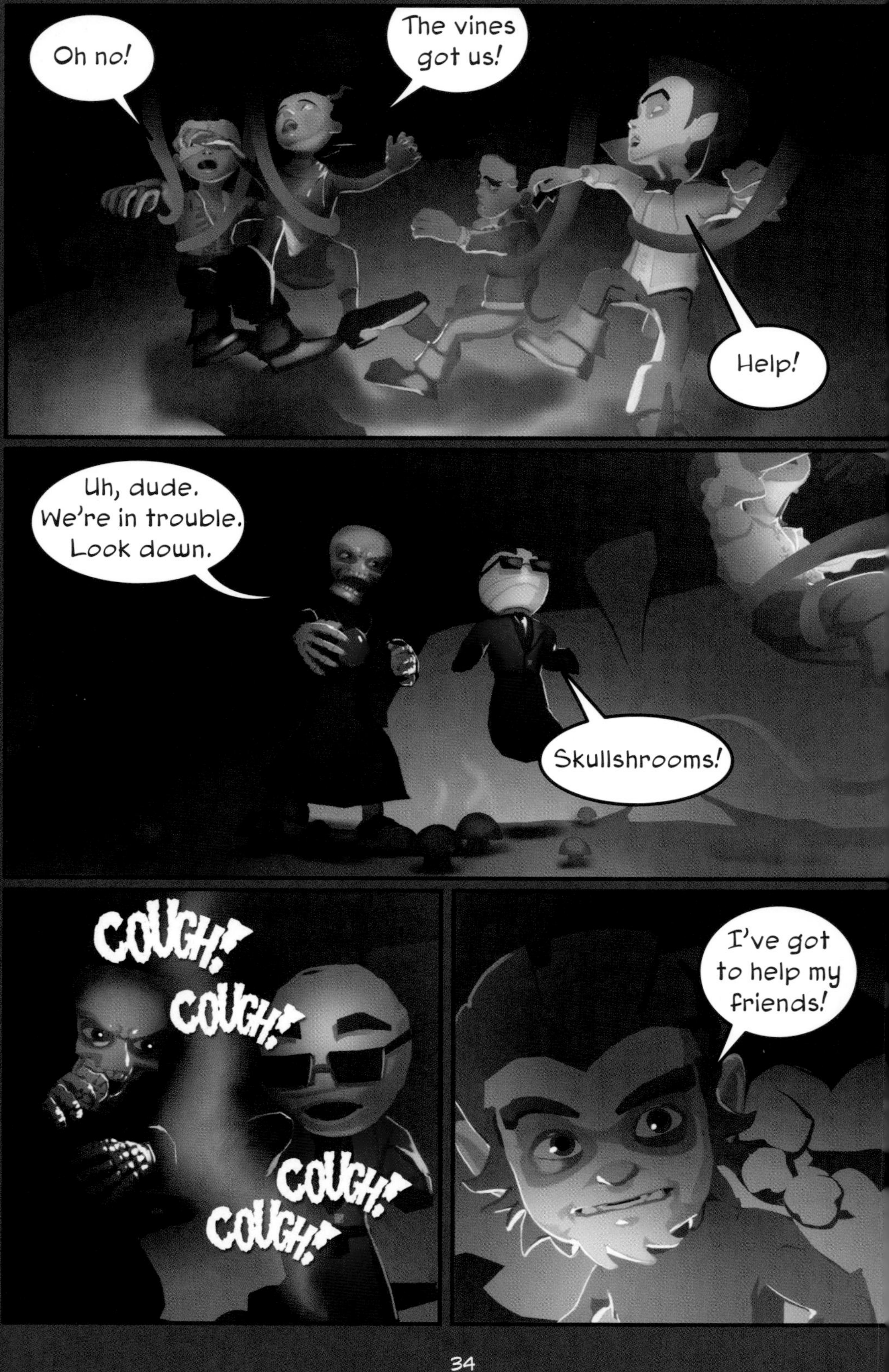
Oh no!
The vines got us!
Help!
Uh, dude. We're in trouble. Look down.
Skullshrooms!
COUGH!
COUGH!
COUGH!
COUGH!
I've got to help my friends!

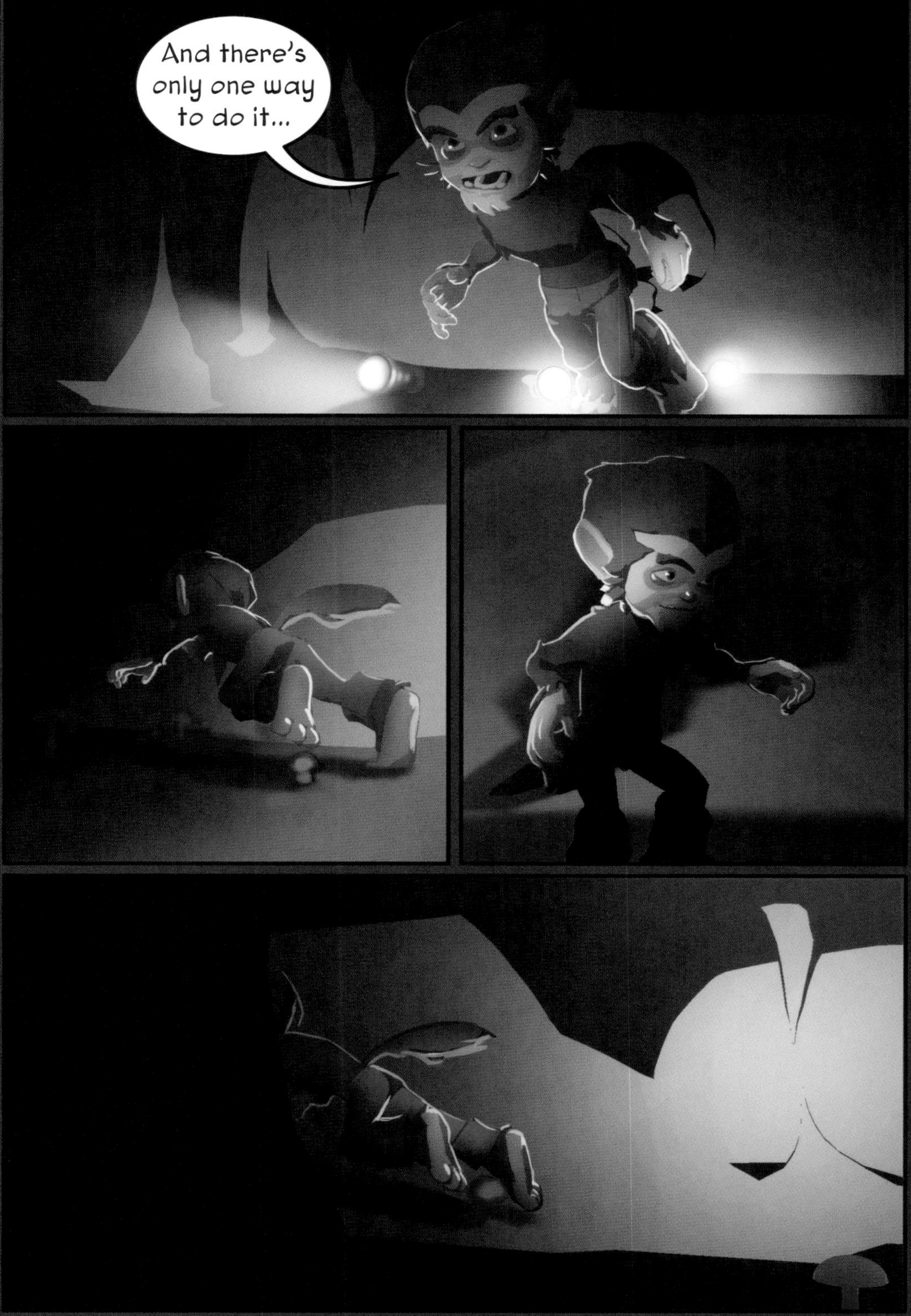
And there's only one way to do it...

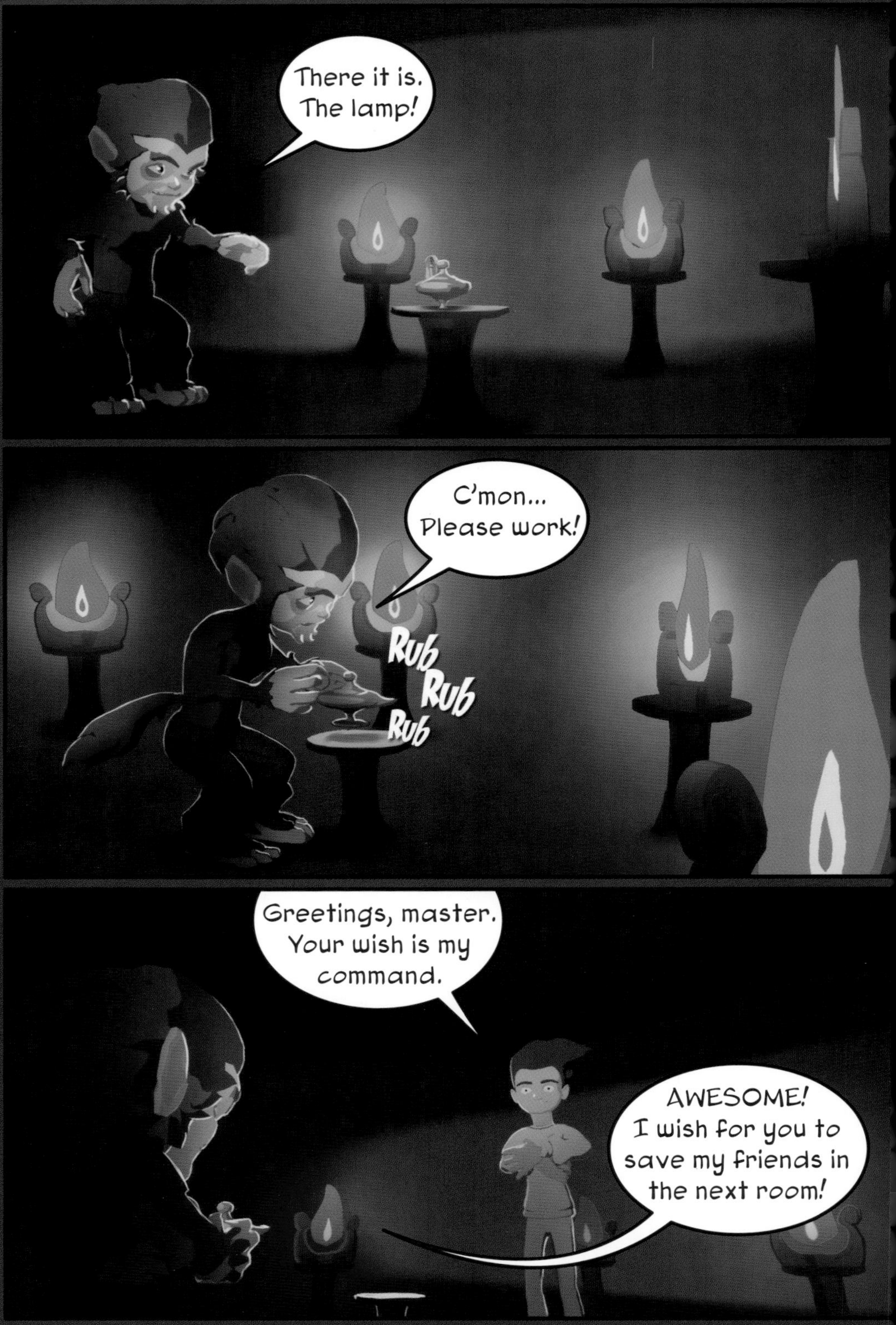
There it is.
The lamp!
C'mon...
Please work!
Rub
Rub
Rub
Greetings, master.
Your wish is my
command.
AWESOME!
I wish for you to
save my friends in
the next room!

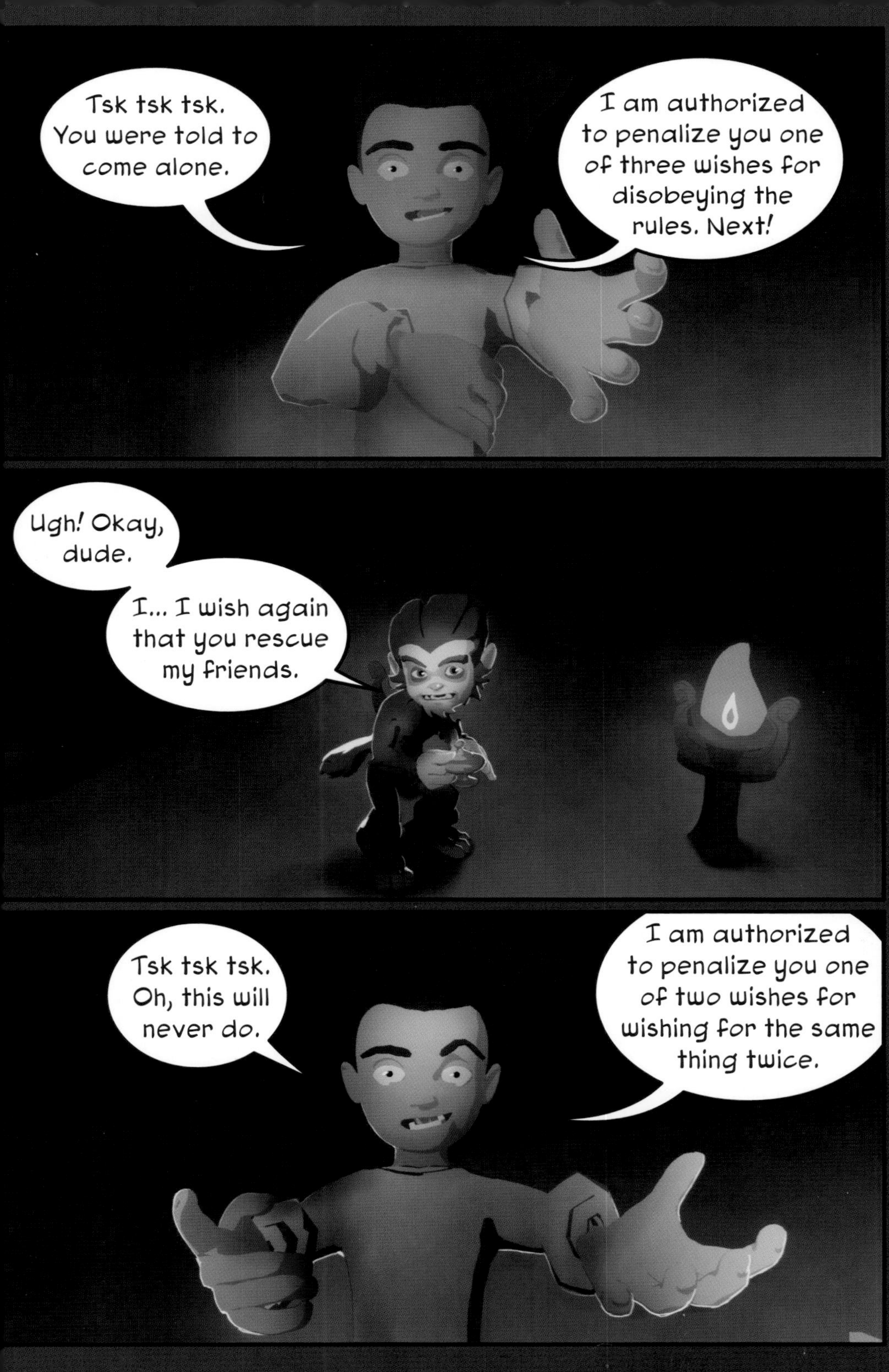
Tsk tsk tsk. You were told to come alone.
I am authorized to penalize you one of three wishes for disobeying the rules. Next!
Ugh! Okay, dude.
I... I wish again that you rescue my friends.
Tsk tsk tsk. Oh, this will never do.
I am authorized to penalize you one of two wishes for wishing for the same thing twice.

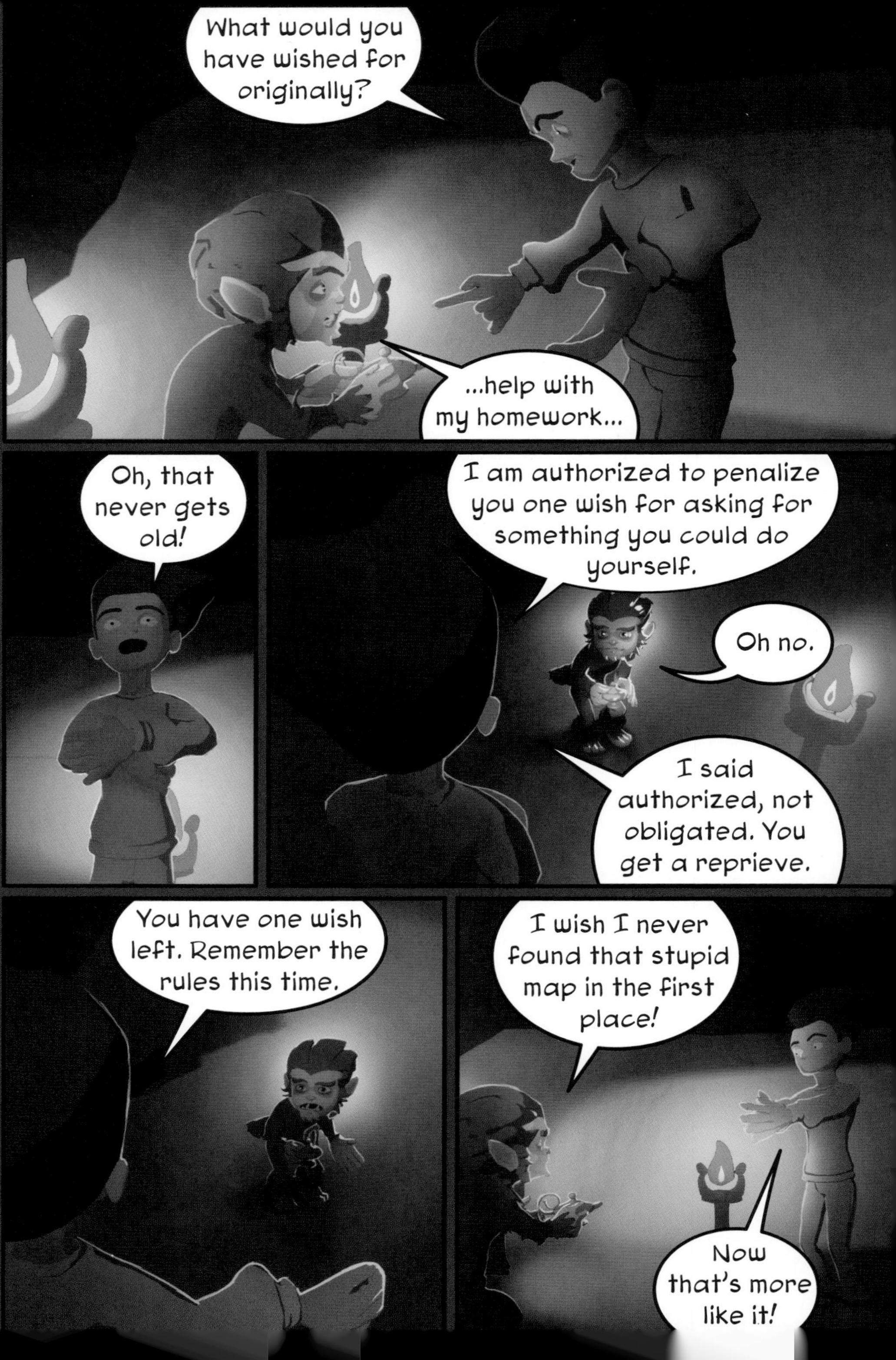
What would you have wished for originally?
...help with my homework...
Oh, that never gets old!
I am authorized to penalize you one wish for asking for something you could do yourself.
Oh no.
I said authorized, not obligated. You get a reprieve.
You have one wish left. Remember the rules this time.
I wish I never found that stupid map in the first place!
Now that's more like it!

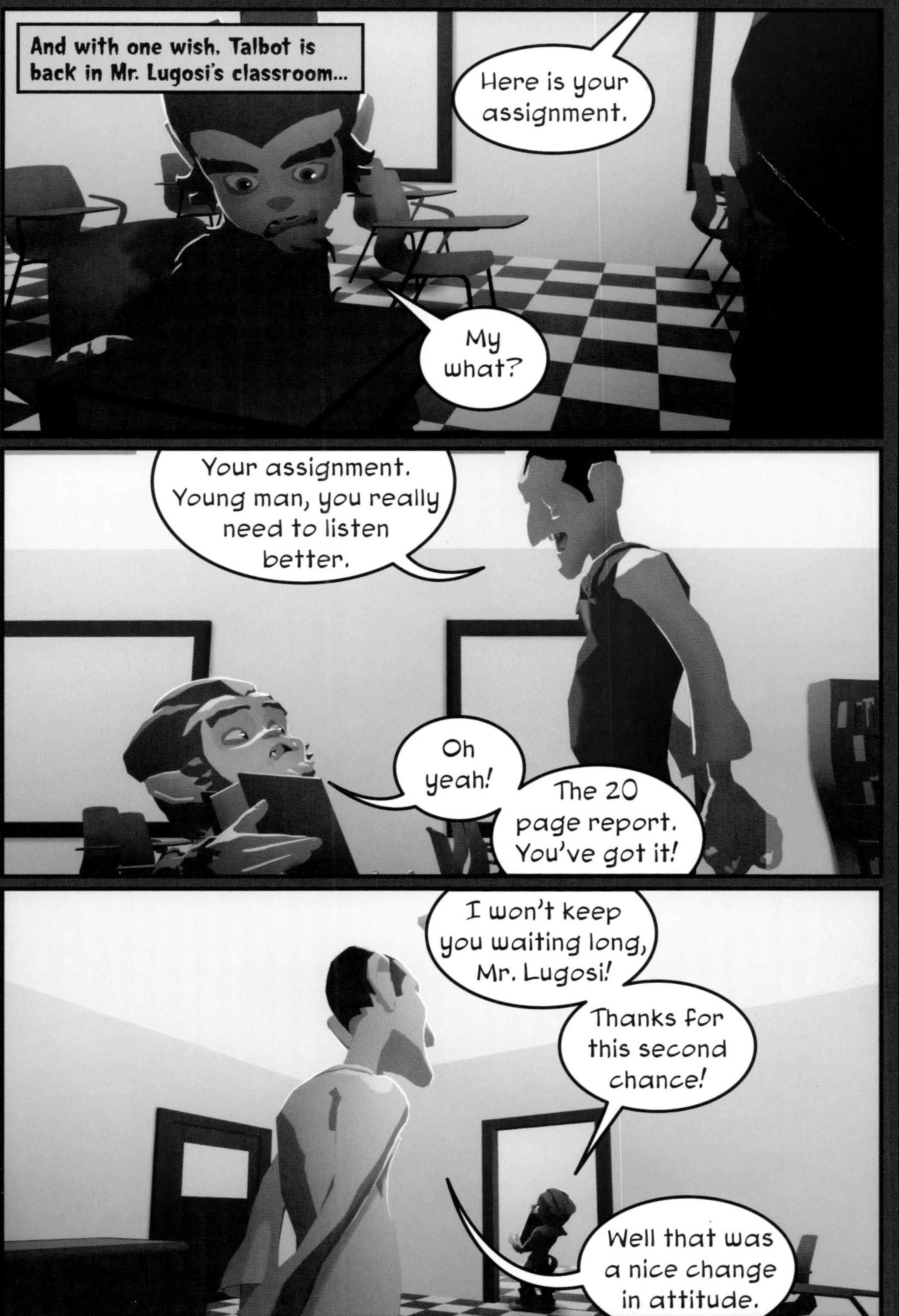
And with one wish, Talbot is back in Mr. Lugosi's classroom...
Here is your assignment.
My what?
Your assignment. Young man, you really need to listen better.
Oh yeah!
The 20 page report. You've got it!
I won't keep you waiting long, Mr. Lugosi!
Thanks for this second chance!
Well that was a nice change in attitude.

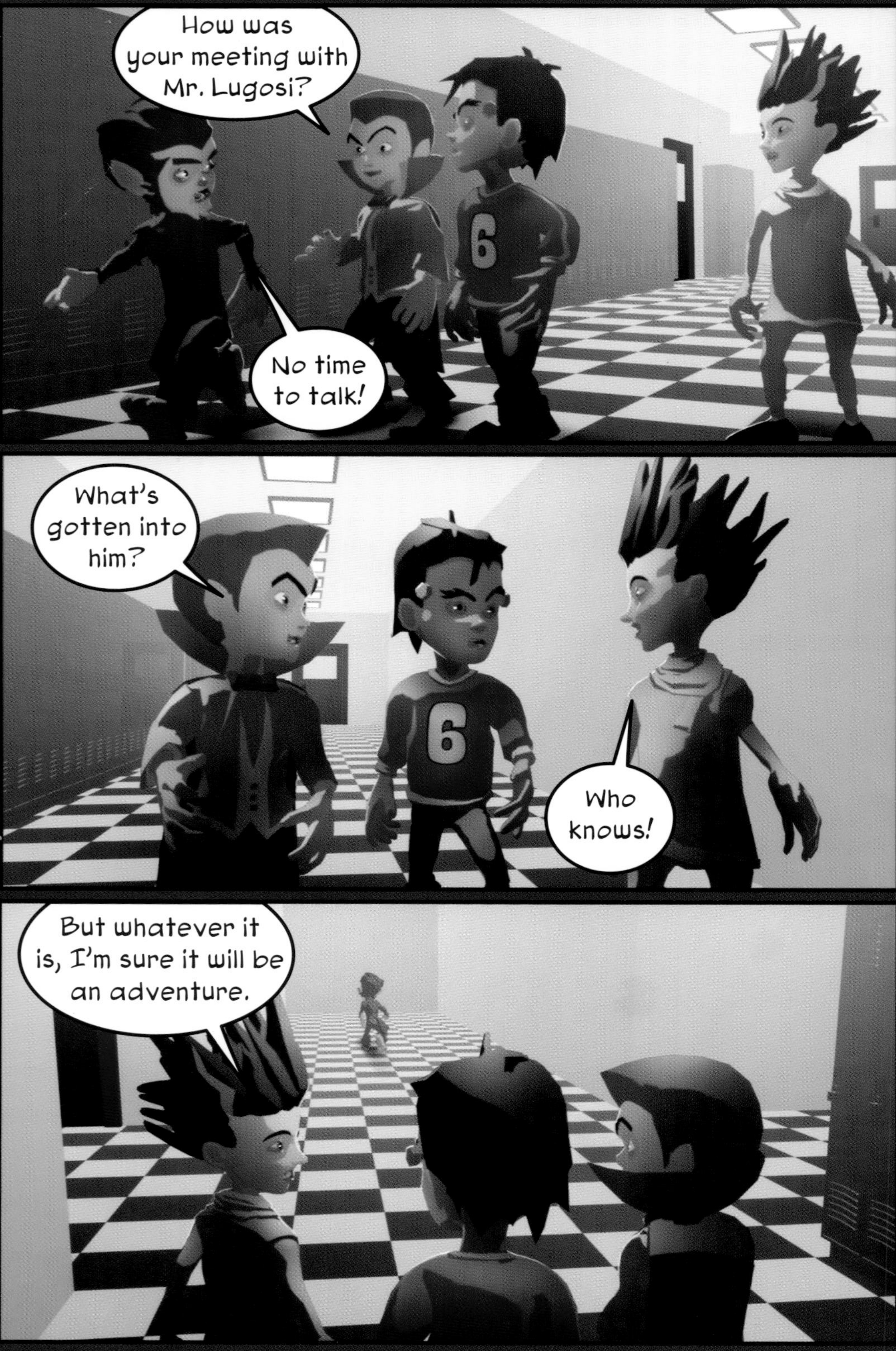
How was your meeting with Mr. Lugosi?
No time to talk!
What's gotten into him?
Who knows!
But whatever it is, I'm sure it will be an adventure.

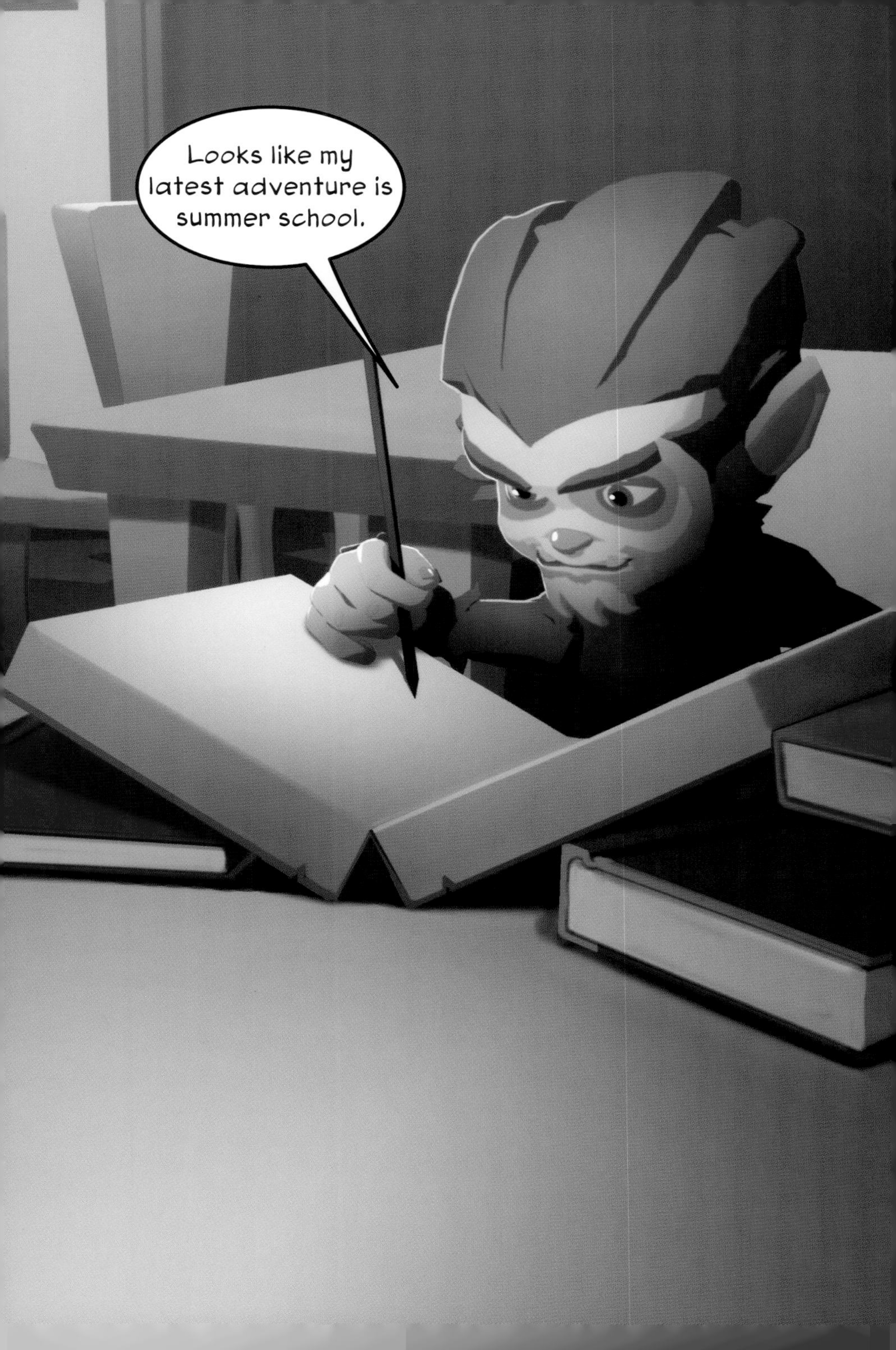
Looks like my latest adventure is summer school.

# THE MAGIC OF
# GENIES

— In Rudyard Kipling's famous story *How the Camel Got His Hump*, a Genie (or Djinn) plays a starring roll. The "Djinn in Charge of All Deserts" is the one who gives the lazy camel his hump.

— Stories featuring genies have been around for hundreds of years, including the popular Arabian Nights tale *The Fisherman and the Genie*.

— In 1965, a popular TV show called *I Dream of Jeannie* began. It featured a pretty blonde genie who was completely in love with her master. It ran for five seasons. Today, shows like *Fairly Odd Parents* and *Wizards of Waverly Place* feature genies and their magical powers.

— In the tale *Aladdin and his Magic Lamp*, the genie grants his master unlimited wishes. In 1992, it became a huge hit movie for Disney under the title of *Aladdin*.

— Famous basketball player Shaquille O'Neal starred as a genie in the 1996 film *Kazaam*. Unlike most genies, he lived in a boombox instead of a magic lamp or bottle.

# GLOSSARY

**authorized** (AW-thuh-rized)—gave official permission for something to happen

**disobeying** (diss-oh-BAY-ing)—going against the rules or someone's wishes

**irresponsible** (ihr-i-SPON-suh-buhl)—reckless and lacking a sense of responsiblility

**obligated** (OB-li-gate-id)—made someone do something because of a law, promise, contract, or sense of duty

**penalize** (PEN-uh-lize)—to make someone suffer a penalty or punishment for something the person has done wrong

**pursue** (pur-SOO)—to continue something

**quest** (KWEST)—a long search

**reprieve** (re-PREEV)—to postpone a punishment

**unacceptable** (uhn-uhk-SEP-tuh-buhl)—not good enough to be allowed or accepted

# DISCUSSION QUESTIONS

1. Because Talbot didn't finish his schoolwork, he had to go to summer school. Do you think that was a fair punishment? Why or why not?

2. Do you think Talbot showed he was responsible by the end of the story? Explain.

3. Were you surprised by the end of the story? Why or why not?

# WRITING PROMPTS

1. Make a list of three things you would wish for if you found a magic lamp.

2. If you found a treasure map, what kind of treasure would you want to find? Write a paragraph describing it.

3. How would you feel if you had to go to summer school? Write a paragraph explaining your feelings.

# ABOUT
# SEAN O'REILLY
## AND ARCANA STUDIO

As a lifelong comics fan, Sean O'Reilly dreamed of becoming a comic book creator. In 2004, he realized that dream by creating Arcana Studio. In one short year, O'Reilly took his studio from a one-person operation in his basement to an award-winning comic book publisher with more than 150 graphic novels produced for Harper Collins, Simon & Schuster, Random House, Scholastic, and others.

Within a year, the company won many awards including the Shuster Award for Outstanding Publisher and the Moonbeam Award for top children's graphic novel. O'Reilly also won the Top 40 Under 40 award from the city of Vancouver and authored The Clockwork Girl for Top Graphic Novel at Book Expo America in 2009. Currently, O'Reilly is one of the most prolific independent comic book writers in Canada. While showing no signs of slowing down in comics, he now writes screenplays and adapts his creations for the big screen.

# Mighty Mighty MONSTERS ADVENTURES

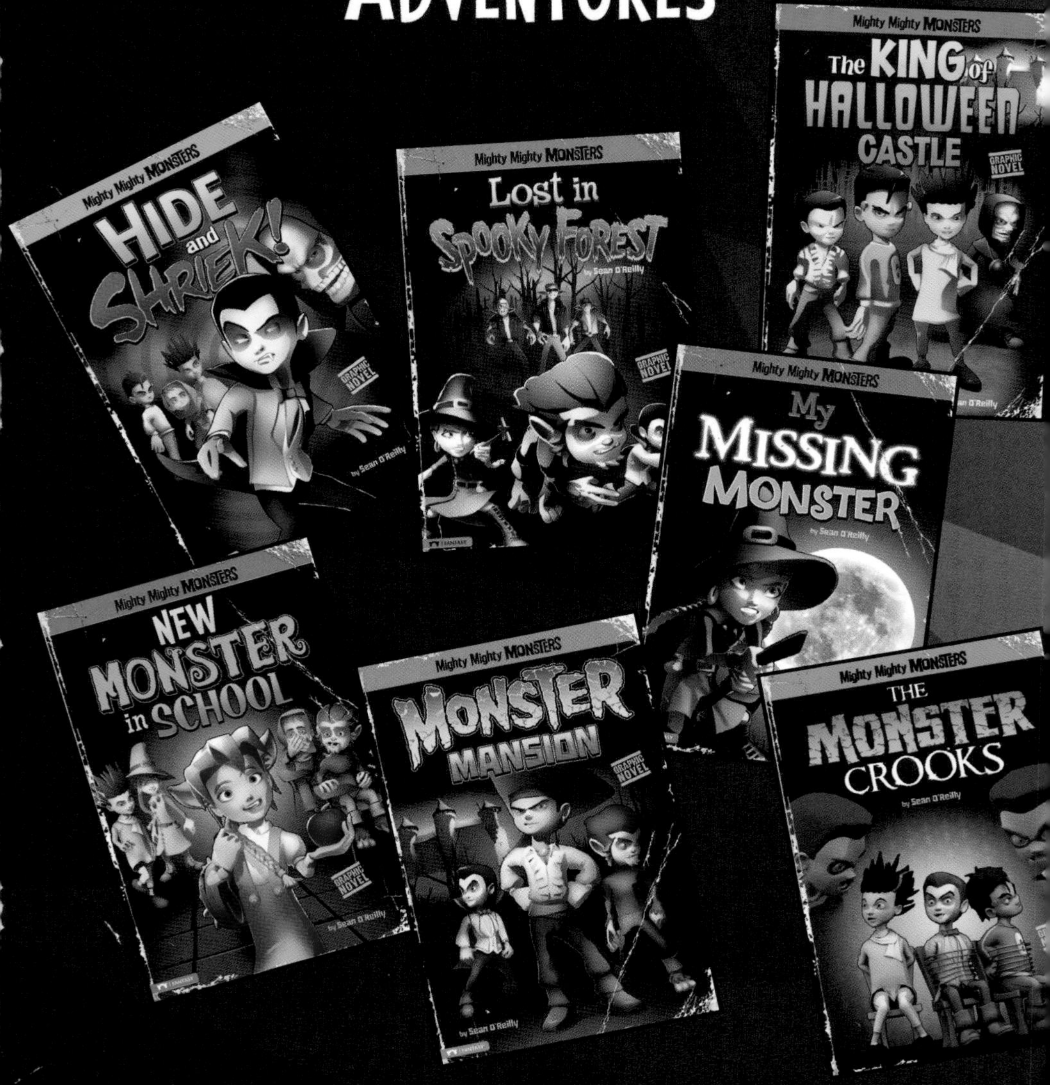
Mighty Mighty MONSTERS
HIDE and SHRIEK!
by Sean O'Reilly
Mighty Mighty MONSTERS
Lost in Spooky Forest
by Sean O'Reilly
Mighty Mighty MONSTERS
The KING of HALLOWEEN CASTLE
Mighty Mighty MONSTERS
My MISSING MONSTER
by Sean O'Reilly
Mighty Mighty MONSTERS
NEW MONSTER in SCHOOL
by Sean O'Reilly
Mighty Mighty MONSTERS
MONSTER MANSION
by Sean O'Reilly
Mighty Mighty MONSTERS
THE MONSTER CROOKS
by Sean O'Reilly

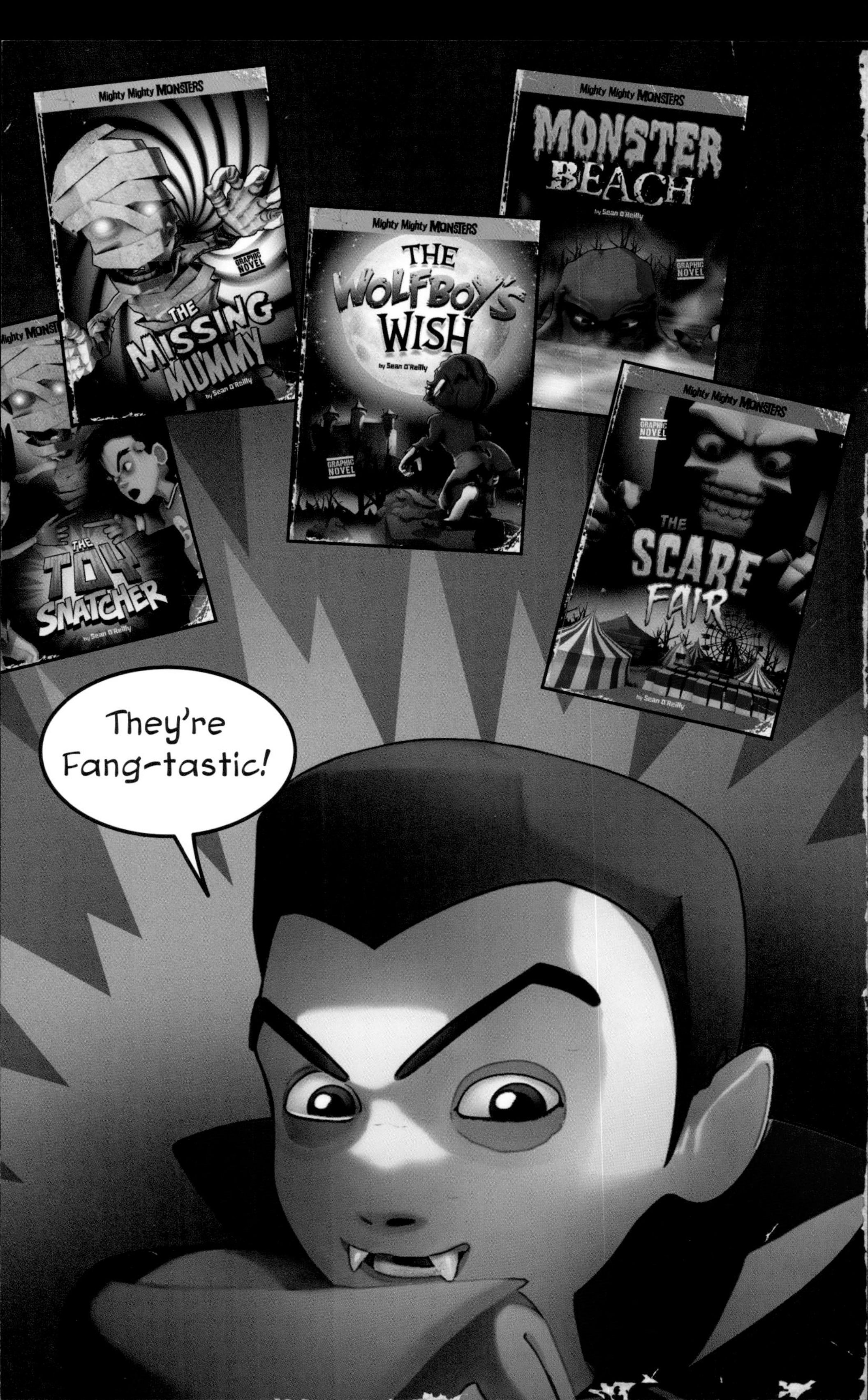
Mighty Mighty MONSTERS
THE MISSING MUMMY
by Sean O'Reilly
GRAPHIC NOVEL
Mighty Mighty MONSTERS
THE WOLFBOY'S WISH
by Sean O'Reilly
GRAPHIC NOVEL
Mighty Mighty MONSTERS
MONSTER BEACH
by Sean O'Reilly
GRAPHIC NOVEL
THE TOY SNATCHER
by Sean O'Reilly
Mighty Mighty MONSTERS
GRAPHIC NOVEL
THE SCARE FAIR
by Sean O'Reilly
They're Fang-tastic!